now and forever

a love story collection

SHIRLEY SIATON

NOW AND FOREVER
A Love Story Collection

Copyright © 2023 Shirley Siaton-Parabia

ALL RIGHTS RESERVED.
No part of this book may be reproduced or used in any manner without the prior written permission of the copyright owner, except for the use of brief quotations in a book review. To request permission, contact the publisher at books@inkysword.com.

This is a work of fiction. Names, characters, businesses, events and incidents are the products of the author's imagination. Any resemblance to actual persons, living or dead, or actual events is purely coincidental.

All brand and product names used in this book are trademarks, registered trademarks, or trade names of their respective owners. Inky Sword Book Publishing is not associated with any product or vendor in this book.

ISBN 978-6-21-490000-8 (pbk)
ISBN 978-6-21-490004-6 (Kindle)

First Edition, September 2023

Published by Shirley S. Parabia

Inky Sword Book Publishing
Barangay Quezon, Arevalo, Iloilo City 5000
Republic of the Philippines
inkysword.com

Content Warnings

Warnings for explicit content, mild profanity, and acts of and references to violence.

Recommended for mature readers 18 years old and above.

Contents

ACKNOWLEDGMENTS ix

THE COLLECTION xi

ONE: assassin 1

TWO: alone 19

THREE: Axis 59

FOUR: Arrival 79

FIVE: Aflame 117

SIX: Angel 129

About the Author 179

Links 180

To the ones who first read these stories in print

ACKNOWLEDGMENTS

This book sprang forth from an idea that my mother, Mimi, came up with during one of our random online chats earlier this year. More specifically, she thought it would be the bee's knees if I shared my short fiction pieces to a wider audience. Well, here you go, Ma.

I am very grateful to Wajahat for patiently transcribing my stories from their original newsprint scans, to Eve of Harbinger Design for the gorgeous book cover, and to Champagne Book Design for formatting this manuscript beautifully.

THE COLLECTION

'Now and Forever' is a special collection of six standalone fiction pieces, each one a romantic short story.

This book was written and compiled over a considerably lengthy creative period, with a massive time jump in the middle. Most of the short stories did not grow into their final incarnation until 2023.

'Assassin,' 'Alone,' 'Arrival' and 'Aflame' kept their original characters from the late 1990s, but placed them in more updated settings.

'Axis' was brought into the 21st century by putting the characters, one of them a visionary OFW, at the forefront of the BPO industry.

'Angel,' the first mature short story I have written, evolved from a simple interaction between two disparate souls in a gritty street corner, taking the form of a darkly poignant love story.

I hope you, my dear reader, will enjoy these tales as much as I relished writing them over the years.

now and forever

a love story collection

ONE

assassin

THE DEN

MORNING CAME WITH A HOWLING WIND, THE KIND that carried dirt and muck that stuck on the skin and never washed out. It seemed to scream in pain.

Arthur gritted his teeth. The storm, gone as quickly as it had come, was over, but everything in the campus was still drenched from the unforgiving intensity of the downpour.

It would be very cold on the field, not to mention muddy. The football pitch looked more like a swamp when he passed by it on his way to the college's main building.

Coach wanted them to start putting in more hours *now*, before first period, for the next intercollegiate football tournament game. Come rain or flood or any other calamity, they would defend their title all the way up to regionals, for the second year in a row.

He descended the steps to the main building's basement. It was a little past six in the morning. The prized player's first class started at eight and now he was most probably in his lair, practicing those deft knee tricks that brought tears to the eyes of the rival coaches.

As team captain, it was Arthur's job to secure the gear and inform the prized player about that morning's practice not getting cancelled in spite of the field's condition.

Not that he'd care either way, he thought bitterly

The prized player was a tireless machine, not a person. He'd show up, do the drills and rounds, and commit the plays to memory. Arthur often wondered what possessed him to turn down the position of captain, after bringing the team to two regional championships since he was a freshman.

Even as a senior, Arthur was only the distant second choice to lead the team this year. His numbers in goals and successful plays were pathetic compared to the prized player's, as was everyone else's. The man pretty much did not miss goals.

He typed in the door code and stepped inside the basement, which housed a collection of old school furniture and relatively new sports equipment. He knocked on the door of a smaller room inside, once a storage closet for cleaning equipment and a break room for campus cleaning staff, before the lay-offs.

This was now the prized player's residence on campus,

because he didn't want to share his space with three other kids in the dormitory next door.

No answer. Arthur turned the knob, finding it unlocked, and pushed warily.

There was nothing in the prized player's room except a sparse wooden cot, an equally drab three-legged table, and a portable clothes rack.

The team helped him load back the equipment only last night, he thought. *Knowing him, he wouldn't move out of this place. It's his lion's den, after all.*

Arthur knew that the prized player had some other stuff around, like dartboards, target posters, and sketches of exotic birds. They were all gone. Nothing was draped on the makeshift clothesline strung across the tiny room.

He stood there and assessed this new information for half a minute.

Arthur took a deep breath and closed the door. He retraced his steps in the basement, retrieving two footballs from the storage racks before he left.

He had better tell Coach that Aragon was gone.

THE DARK

Dawn.

He gingerly lowered his body onto the lopsided stone bench overlooking the quad. His muscles ached and his sides burned from the run.

The campus was still cloaked in darkness. He had been running for more than an hour, but the sky still resembled a blue-black canopy strewn with darker masses of clouds. Not a ray of sunlight breached his limited view of the horizon. The air was thick and heavy, and sullied by city dust.

Rain was coming.

He felt a detached, perverse satisfaction.

"Aragon?"

A female voice had said his family name. People knew him by that name.

Aragon. A name full of history. His place of birth was far enough away, but he could still recollect the smells of gunpowder, the crisp click of a gun's hammer, the echo of death cries. They all came with his heritage.

His well-trained eyes made out her silhouette. The lighting in the campus was limited and the few functional lampposts badly needed their bulbs replaced.

"Jeri." Her name fell from his lips. After all this time, he was still surprised at the way he would say it. Softer, slower than his usual speech, and always with awe.

She was dressed in a white top with her jean shorts. The wind played with the strands of her long hair. She carried a black duffel bag, the size of which dwarfed her frame.

He wasn't surprised to feel his chest tighten, his heartbeat accelerate. "What are you doing here? How did you get in the campus?"

He watched her place the bag on the concrete pavement

and take a seat beside him. Her eyes, always strangely luminous, flickered in the semi-darkness.

"I had to see you," she replied simply.

"How did you get in?" he pressed.

He lived on campus, in the main building's basement. He had first lodged in a boarding house, then moved to the dormitory after he secured a permanent spot in the college's varsity football team. He hated the noise and the activity of shared living spaces.

Coach had allowed him to hole up in the old janitors' break room, right next to the storage where sports teams kept all their equipment. The older man could not refuse the simple request of the college's star athlete and pulled every string he could with Administration to make this strange request happen.

"There are benefits to being part of the Student Council." There was a smile in her voice. "I couldn't sleep. I figured you would be here."

"Yes. I couldn't sleep either. As always, the best option is to run."

He opened his arms and she snuggled into them. She pressed her face to his chest, not minding his sweat-soaked shirt.

"You should eat more," she said.

"Really?"

"Yes. I don't know where you get all that energy to move so fast, or to kick that hard." Her breath whispered through the worn material of his shirt. "Or to run so much every day."

"I don't know. Habit, maybe."

They both lapsed into silence. In the darkness, she reached for his hands. He felt her delicate skin brush against his scarred and callused palms.

Even though they were much, much closer than people expected them to be, he had never once stopped marveling at how they appeared to be so different from each other.

She was the epitome of intelligence and charisma. Everyone liked her—from the teachers, to the cafeteria staff, even the freshmen and the super-seniors. She always had that ready smile and the time to listen to everyone's problems. People believed that sleeping wasn't on her busy schedule; that Jeri Castelo would rather stay up talking to someone in her trademark high-octane and witty manner, organizing events as a member of the Supreme Student Council, or tutoring younger students in Calculus.

He was popular in another fashion: the star football player who never gave away much about himself. The name Aragon struck fear in the teams of colleges all over the region. Ever since his freshman year, he had brought the university an unprecedented steady stream of championships.

He was not, however, raised to become an athletic achiever. His training had aimed to accomplish more serious ends.

Deadly serious ends.

In his first year, their class had gone on a trip up the mountains as part of their Biology subject. While everyone had lugged bags of canned goods and other packaged foods, he had only brought clothes and minimal camping equipment. Evening at their campsite, the teacher had asked, "Where's the dinner you're supposed to bring for yourself?"

"It's right behind you, sir." He had thrown his hunting knife, the blade whizzing a mere inch above his professor's head.

A wild chicken, an *ilahas*, had squawked and crashed to the ground in rapid succession. He then had an entire roasted chicken for his dinner, served hot. No one shared his meal, or spoke to him for the rest of the trip. The teacher gave him a grade of 1.0.

After that, everyone dealt with him very cautiously. No one dared to test his temper, even though he had never once displayed it, on or off the field.

He liked things that way. The further he distanced himself, the better.

Only Jeri had dared break through the wall between him and the rest of the world.

During the college mixer party at the start of their sophomore year, she had asked him to dance, locating him in the shadows of the auditorium. He had been standing in a corner, nearly undetectable as far as he was concerned. He was fond of honing his stealth skills, but she had made him realize his abilities at the time were rather rusty, if not questionable.

Jeri Castelo, one of the most popular girls in school, was actually standing right there and asking him to dance with her.

The varicolored strobe lights of the darkened building had accentuated the spark of recklessness in her eyes.

He had been very flustered. "I don't know how to—"

"Aragon, if you turn me down, I will kill you."

In that very moment, he fell in love with her.

THE CONFESSION

That was more than a year ago.

He had fallen hard and fast.

She had not been of any help, either. She had wanted him, too.

At the end of the night they first danced, she had taken his hand, led him to the darkened, empty backstage area of the auditorium, and kissed him.

He had kissed her back, among other things. He had tried to find his way through their sweaty clothing and bodies, her scent of cologne, something fruity and warm, undeniably overpowering his reason and control. She had tasted of something fruity and warm, too, all of her.

Since then, he had been unable to distance himself or stop thinking about her, no matter how hard he tried.

She had been his first, in so many ways.

Nobody knew anything about what went on between them. It had been a perfectly hidden secret, until the time Lexie, Jeri's best friend, had seen them kissing in an empty classroom before the citywide football championship last year.

But whatever Lexie saw was never mentioned. He

understood why she and Jeri were best friends; they kept each other's secrets without question.

"The first time I saw you, you were practicing alone in the field," Jeri was now saying. "It was raining, but you never even missed a goal. You were wearing this exact same shirt. It was kind of new then."

He smiled in the darkness. Only very few had seen him smile.

She felt the slight chuckle rumbling through his chest. "What the hell are you so amused about?"

"You." He pulled her closer. Jeri's frame fitted his bigger one snugly. "Why do you always have to be so *perfect*? You remember, know, and do almost everything."

Her breathing seemed to stop. It took moments before she could answer. "I was raised to be like that. No one could make up for my mistakes, if I was stupid enough to make them. When I moved in with my grandparents after my parents died, I learned this very quickly."

She paused, as if gathering momentum. "When I was little, my grandmother would slap my hands with a stick whenever I couldn't spell a word correctly. Or, sometimes, they wouldn't let me have dinner unless I could recite an entire speech without any mistakes. I got good at all of it. Then better. By the time I was eight, there was no more need for such discipline. I delivered everything they wanted."

"When I got older, my grandparents told me my

mother failed them by eloping with my father. She had me when she was eighteen. And I…I couldn't fail my family."

The words had a pained, bitter edge. He could taste them in his own heart. If there was someone who understood, only too well, how it was like to rise to the nearly impossible expectations and demands of their family, it was him.

"It gets exhausting. I'm doing a great job at it, though. There are so many people expecting so many things. I had to do all those things. I feel guilty when I couldn't. Sometimes it's like digging your own grave. But you need to do it anyway." Her voice sounded rough and strained. "Being perfect was the only way to survive, to keep having value."

The first few raindrops fell. He felt them on his arm. Then he realized they weren't from the sky. The droplets were her tears. In all the time he had known Jeri, this was the first time he had seen her cry.

Something bubbled inside him. It wasn't rage, but a calmer desire to kill. It was part of him, his lifeblood. Although he had vowed to himself never to take a human life again, he would break that for her in a heartbeat.

But there was no one entirely responsible for that sort of torment she felt. Just like no one had to pay for his past, except perhaps he himself.

"I'm sorry…" His voice trailed off. He felt lame and helpless, as a familiar cold numbness ran the length of his spine. It was a feeling only pulling the trigger could relieve.

"I shouldn't have said–"

"It's not your fault. Sometimes I just couldn't help but think about this, no matter how hard I try not to." She bravely swallowed back her sobs as he wiped her tears away. "I had it coming. I had it coming all these years. It was only a matter of time before I got burned out."

He waited for her to calm down. She could so easily collect herself, or at least appear to have done so. He was the only one who would always know and feel the trembling of her hands, the uneven beating of her pulse, even if she appeared perfectly composed.

She had looked like this during debates when she ran for the student council, when after she felt as cold as ice to his touch. Everyone else had praised her composure and quick thinking, never considering the amount of control it took on her part.

"I was raised to be the best, too," he said, slowly, cautiously. "I became the best."

Jeri's tearstained face had a look that showed the struggle to comprehend his words. She said nothing, but spoke volumes with wide eyes.

He knew at that point he had to explain, to make her understand.

"When I was in high school, I was known as Cain in the underground. My father chose that name for me. I was born with a twin brother, but my cord was around his neck when we were cut out…I choked him to death in our mother's womb."

"I didn't know…" She was groping for words. "You never—"

He squeezed her hands in his, shaking his head slightly, feeling his lips turn in that slight, almost imperceptible smile he could give to no one but her.

It was his way of telling her it was okay. He would be okay, if he had her with him.

"I'm the youngest of five brothers, but I could outshoot all of them. I could take them all down hand to hand, too, by the time I was seven. I was faster and stronger. I was even better in most sports. A lot of schools offered everything from bribes to scholarship packages to my parents so I would go to their place, just so they could get all the football titles, even a national games medal."

"My father then told us that the mantle of the Eagle-Eye had to be passed down. He was almost sixty and it was about time for him to mentor the next one. All my uncles—everyone in my family—wanted me to take it. I was fourteen. The Eagle-Eye tattoo meant the world."

"That explains the eagle mark on your chest." Jeri placed her hand over his heart. "It's more than just a tattoo."

"Our family has been in the Philippines for more than three hundred years. You can say we wrote a lot of history in blood and no one ever knew. We are loyal to no one, except our own kin and land. That's how we had roots. The

Eagle-Eye is the best of the present generation. He was entrusted to carry out the most dangerous missions."

He said everything without any pride. Then again, there was nothing to be proud of.

A series of frozen frames flashed in his memory. He drew in a sharp breath at how vividly he could remember the events of seven years past.

"My initiation rite was to kill a priest who had sexually abused the son of one of our workers at the corn farm. The boy was eight, a *sacristan*. It was three-thirty in the morning…the priest was walking to Church to prepare for the *misa de gallo*. I got him with one shot, right between the eyes. It was Christmas—and my fifteenth birthday—when I became the ninth-generation Eagle-Eye. That's when I got the tattoo. Then my father said, 'You will be Cain now.'"

"There are twenty-nine others on my list; two of them were very young, maybe seven or eight years old. They were the children of a drug lord who thought he could smuggle *shabu* through one of the canning companies in our town. They saw me shoot their father. *Leave no witnesses*. That was in the rules."

"You killed people." Her voice was toneless. Not angry, afraid or accusing, just clear and audible.

"I left Surallah thinking I could somehow lose that part of me. I bargained for four years to finish college so there's time to think about it. No matter how hard you try, that side of you stays right where it is. If you try to get rid of it somehow, it will eat you up alive. You could shed your skin, but not your blood. You wouldn't have the strength to survive."

He realized she had not backed away, or showed any sign of fear or disgust.

Before he could say anything more, she looked straight into his eyes, unblinking. He could see the clarity in her gaze, behind the sheen of tears, in the soft light of the oncoming sunrise.

"I love you, Nick. Nothing's going to change that."

Nick.

His Christian name was Nicholas, but no one called him that. It was always Aragon to everyone else.

She was the only one who called him by that name.

The absence of revulsion from her took him aback. "I know I should have told you before. I couldn't, Jeri. I didn't want to lose you. I'm so sorry—"

"There's nothing to be sorry for." Her tone was firm, although she spoke in a voice so quiet it was almost carried away by the early morning breeze. "I loved you for what you are. I found in you a part of myself I thought I'd never find in anyone else."

He swallowed hard, ice and dread gripping his insides. "You're not angry, are you?"

She shook her head. "Why should I be? Because you told me the truth?"

"But I'm a…*killer*. You should be walking away right now."

Jeri did the exact opposite.

She put her arms around him. "I'm staying right here. I'm not going anywhere. Don't you know how good it feels to finally hear you talk about where you came from?"

"Jeri, I…" His voice trailed off. He had no words for her. He only had himself and everything else.

She took his hand and placed it gently on her belly. "I love you for being the father of this child."

It took him a second to understand what she meant by both her actions and words. When he finally did, he felt all the air leave his lungs.

He could only stare at her as a sudden glow began to form in the pit of his stomach. It was the familiar warmth he had known only when he met her.

When he finally mustered some semblance of self-control, he said, "Are you…?"

He couldn't finish the question. The idea was too unreal, too beautiful, to speak of. Part of him feared it would disappear right before his eyes, along with her.

Instead, she smiled brightly. "Maybe six weeks now. A doctor who doesn't know my family confirmed it yesterday afternoon. That's why I had to see you. I could no longer keep this a secret." Her face, so breathtakingly beautiful to him, was a study in mixed emotions. "I had to tell you."

"I'm going to be a father," he said slowly, tasting the word. He put his hands on her stomach, over her own. His own blood, now with hers.

Father, he repeated inwardly. A father.

She nodded.

This time, the first real drops of rain started to fall.

A droplet landed on his lips. He tasted sweetness and warmth. It bore none of the bitter taste and spilled blood of the past three hundred years.

A bolt of lightning streaked across the sky, followed by a loud rumble of thunder, just before the rain came down in earnest.

In silent agreement, neither of them suggested taking shelter in the nearby gazebos surrounding the campus quad.

Jeri stepped back and spread out her arms, giggling as she turned her face up to the downpour.

As he watched her spinning slowly under the rain, he realized that he was still half-stunned by her news.

She paused for a moment, her movements punctuated by a soft giggle. "Nick, I want to dance with you."

In that moment, his head cleared, as if someone had shone a light on the shadows of his burden. He took her hands in his and placed her palms over his heart, on the very same spot where his body bore the Eagle-Eye mark. "I love you."

She smiled and stood on tiptoe, pressing her lips to his. "For the first time in our lives, let's not be the best assassin or the perfect girl. Let's do the right thing and just be us."

He nodded. "Us," he repeated, trying the sound of the word rolling off his tongue. He liked the ring of it.

The rain fell harder.

He basked in the sight of the woman who had looked

him in the eye and never wavered, even after his confession and the deaths he had brought.

Instead, she embraced him and his blood.

She looked straight back at him, the same way she had the night of their first dance. The night she'd opened the door to his heart and, unwittingly, to his freedom from the shadows of the past.

Nicholas Aragon embraced her then.

Nothing more was said.

The rain crashed around them, drenching concrete, earth, steel, and their bodies.

When the sun finally rose, the thunderstorm came to an end. Only the wind was left howling, singing a dirge to the shadows as they became one with the light.

THE LETTER

It was Lexie's habit, for the past two years now, to drop by the newspaper office every morning to check on messages and writing assignments.

When she arrived, on the dot, at half-past seven, the first thing she noticed was a folded note tacked to the corkboard. Her name was on it, in a familiar roundish script.

She took the paper off the board and unlocked the door.

The note felt slightly damp in her hands as she

unfolded it. The paper seemed to have gotten wet in the heavy rain earlier that morning and was slowly drying out.

My dearest Lexie,

I've held on for years to what I thought I was.

I have become the perfect puppet to expectations that were never mine. It's time to cut the strings.

I gave them my entire life, until now. From today, it's my turn to live the rest of it on my own terms.

I will miss you.

Love always,

Jeri

She stared at the signature. Like her best friend's personality, it had an undeniable, inimitable flourish.

For a long time, Lexie stood in the middle of the empty office, her gaze seeing beyond the unlit space before her.

She went through the drafts left on the table for her to review, locked up, and headed to her first class of the day.

Along the way, she stopped by one of the trash cans on the quad and tore the letter to shreds. She watched the tiny white pieces fall from her hands like raindrops disappearing into the cold morning air.

"Be happy, Jeri," she whispered. "I'll miss you, too."

TWO

alone

H E WAS PREDICTABLE, AND SHE LIKED IT THAT WAY. With Vincent Tugade, she always knew where she stood, what to expect. Everything about him was practically routine.

That morning, she immediately knew, the moment she saw a small box of cookies on her desk, that he was back. He had spent most of t he past two months working offsite in Pampanga, in rounds of audits to wrap up the tax year. Although he wasn't the only auditor who had traveled there, she knew he was the only one who would remember to get her a gift, usually a sampling of the local delicacies.

Katrina David smiled and, delightedly, made her way across the building floor, from Human Resources to the side of the external auditors, which everyone in their firm called Assassins' Block.

Vincent's office was at a far corner, smaller than most but with an expansive view of Pasay City. The walls were almost bare except for a few framed certificates and photographs. It was always scented with the strong black coffee he drank all the time.

He was seated behind his two computer screens when she walked in. He looked up when he saw her. He jumped to his feet and swooped down on her for a hug.

"Welcome back, VAT," she said, putting her arms around him.

Years ago, when he first joined the firm, she had found his initials to be a little too fitting for his profession. As a result, she began using it. Then it stuck.

His familiar warmth was always comforting, as was the cool, subtle scent of his cologne.

"You look so brown. Eaten one too many plates of *sisig*?"

He laughed as he kissed her on the check. "Jealous much? It's good to be back. How have you been, Trina?"

"It's been busy around here," she said, giving him a peck in return. "I had no one to complain to these past few months, though. You missed a lot."

Vincent Alcon Tugade was the poster boy for yuppie Manila. He had classic Filipino looks, from his brown skin to his proud face with the hard planes, broad nose and dark eyes. He always dressed simply and elegantly, in light shirts and dark slacks, with hair neatly combed back. He appeared trustworthy and competent, without being obnoxious about any of it.

"I'm sure I did," he said. "With you around, I'll catch up in no time."

She sat on one of the chairs in front of his desk, one leg folded under her, and leaned forward. "How are you? Did anything exciting happen in Pampanga?"

"If you call spending fourteen hours a day with ledgers exciting, by all means, it was very exciting. I had the time of my life."

"You're no fun, Vince."

"You're welcome to all the fun, Trina." His smile at her was nothing if not indulgent, like a patient adult to a restless child. "I'll stick to my balance sheets. I don't think I've got energy for much else."

She frowned at him, exasperated but unsurprised. If he wasn't Vincent, she would have felt patronized. They were about the same age, but she had long since accepted that he behaved like a much older man. Her own father, who was into Airsoft and war games tournaments, was more fun than him.

She pouted at him. "Well, you'd better have enough energy to dance at my wedding, at least."

His hand froze over the computer mouse, just as one of his eyebrows shot up into his hairline. It took a second before he said anything.

"Abella asked?"

"He's going to." Trina saw he was about to say something more, but she stopped him by interrupting. "Soon. Maybe this weekend. We're having dinner on Saturday night. He's pulling out all the stops, VAT. Five-star hotel, the works."

She watched him lean back in his chair.

Broad-shouldered, well spoken, neat, and fairly easy to fit in the bill of tall, dark and handsome, he would have been very cute, she thought objectively, had he not been so boring.

Mature, she corrected herself, loyally. *He's just mature.*

"Well, in exchange for the cookies, I'm claiming first dibs on the happy news."

Trina stood up and rolled her eyes. She would have liked to stay if not for their department's Monday morning meeting.

"I've got to go for our team meeting. I never knew those cookies had a price, though."

"Miss David, you have worked for this firm your entire professional life." He switched to what she called his Presentation Mode, which he usually assumed in meetings with clients. It was the most deathly serious and, somehow, also one of the most comical voices she'd ever heard. "You should know by now that everything has a price."

Maybe he wasn't so boring, after all.

It was Saturday.

He picked up a dart from the coffee table in the middle of his apartment, aimed, and took the shot. The dart found its target, a small square of paper he had tacked to his reminders board.

Vincent walked up to the board and removed the dart. It had pierced right through the piece of desk calendar for that month, exactly where he had intended it to.

Today. *Saturday.*

He woke up that morning the same time he did every day, at five sharp. His apartment was close to Pasay City Sports Complex, so on most days he would go for a run. Today was no different.

After his run, he returned to his place and cooked oatmeal and eggs for breakfast. If he was not working weekends or on travel somewhere, he preferred staying in. If he had the chance, he would go out on Friday and Saturday nights.

Tonight, he definitely was going out. He needed to get out.

He had received the announcement the night before, at eleven, by text message.

R1: 100% Stock Engine & Chassis

R2: Stock 4Stroke

R3: Stock 4Stroke Automatic

R4: Open to All Brands & Models

Track: Legal confirm 8PM Sat 22/4

Entry: TBC msg 9PM Sat 22/4

Vincent Tugade was a drag racer in the Manila underground circuit. His moniker, for many years now, was the King of Chains, from the insignia on the hood of his glistening black Dodge, paired with his signature leather clothing of the same color. His father had sketched this design for a race car back in the day; he had taken it upon himself to bring it to life.

He was into cars as far back as he could remember, spending long hours with his father at their garage during weekends, learning as much as he could about automobile design and engines.

Although his father had been a government tax official, his passion was customizing cars, which he had passed on to his son.

Vincent had been racing since he was eighteen, two years after his parents died from a freak traffic accident that involved a drunk driver ramming his pick-up truck into their own car. It was a bitter, ugly kind of irony.

He had uprooted himself and his little sister Veronica, ten years old at the time, from their province, and came to Metro Manila to live with one of their aunts, who taught at a Catholic private school. He had worked at the school as an errand boy at first, which led to the discovery of his near-prodigious understanding of numbers when he balanced the books of the school cafeteria and the uniform shop in less than a week.

Around the time, one of his jobs at his aunt's house was to look after her car, an ancient orange Toyota with manual transmission. He had been searching for a replacement for the stick shift at one of the shops in Makati when he overheard two men discussing an upcoming 'race.' That had piqued his curiosity in no time. Not long after, he had secretly souped up his aunt's ToyoPet and brought it for a run at an open race one night in late summer, just before he was due to start college.

By the time he graduated and got an Accountancy degree, he had garnered enough supporters and winnings to get his own car. An auditor's job allowed him more financial freedom to support his sister through university, buy a second car, and lease-to-own the condominium he now lived in.

Two years ago, his aunt had passed away quietly from a long-term illness. His little sister, after years of looking after their aunt, had decided to put her Nursing degree to good use and returned to their home province to take a high-profile clinical instructor job.

The glorious bachelor life allowed him to work as much as he liked with numbers during the day and race as much as he wanted at night. It was a simple delineation of the things he was good at.

He was on his second cup of coffee and was about to go downstairs to the parking basement to check his car for the night's race when his phone rang.

The name on the screen was the least expected of all. The presence of Katrina David was the only fluctuating value in the perfectly balanced books of his work and personal life.

He picked up the call.

"Hello, Trina." He tried to keep his voice as neutral as possible. "How are you?"

To his surprise, the response at the other end of the line was not the usual exuberant one he was familiar with.

"Hi, Vince. I'm so sorry for bothering you. Did I call at a bad time?"

It was Trina, but she sounded so subdued it was like he was talking to an entirely different person.

"No, not at all. Everything okay?"

"You got a minute to talk? Please?"

No nicknames, no jokes, no comments on the absence of fun in his life. Maybe he had somehow wandered into a more depressing alternate reality after his early-morning run.

"Sure, of course. Anything for you." He took a seat on his couch. "What's up?"

"Nothing." There was a long, strained pause from her. "I mean, not nothing, but it's something I can't talk about with my parents or my friends."

"I'm all ears. What's this about?"

"James."

"Abella?"

The prick?

He wanted to tack on his opinion, but decided to keep his mouth shut.

The thought of James Abella, Trina's boyfriend, gave him the sudden urge to punch something. Vincent disliked him the same way he disliked racers who would rather spend money on a custom paint job than change their engine oil after a few races.

He had only met Abella three times at office functions over the past year or so but had long since formed the impression that the man was all flash, no substance. Perhaps a career in modeling did that to a person, but Vincent never generalized and only gave informed opinions. Since Trina was not a client, he kept whatever sentiments he had to himself.

"Has he done something? Are you okay?"

"Nothing like that. I'm fine."

He tried to be patient, thinking of the way he would usually talk to his little sister when she opened up about her relationships. "Okay, then, Trina. Just let me know if there's anything I can do."

Maybe, just maybe, run Abella over. She could pick which car I should use.

"Vince…what happens if I don't want to?"

"Don't want to what?"

"You know. The S-word."

He almost sputtered on his coffee. He slowly put his mug down on the table to avoid any further incident.

Damn. So much for your regular Saturday morning routine.

He held the phone away from his mouth as he took a deep breath before responding.

"I thought everything was done, dusted and double-ruled, all that. He was going to ask you to marry him, wasn't he?"

"He wants to take our relationship further, has wanted to for a while now. If he does ask me tonight to marry him and I say yes, he might want a…"

"Test drive?" He completed the statement and immediately regretted it.

"Yes." Deadpan and humorless, Trina had probably been

replaced by an alien who happened to mimic her voice very well.

The silence on the line stretched for what seemed like hours.

There was only one response he could utter, the only one that mattered.

"What do you want to do?"

He heard a huge intake of breath, before she continued in a shaky voice. "I don't know. That's why I called you, to ask a man how he would feel if his fiancée refused to…you know."

This was dangerous ground. He would never speak for the prick.

"Has he asked you before?" He swallowed very hard before continuing. "Have you done it with him before?"

Fuck.

He could feel it. His face was going red. He was supposed to give advice on depreciation and inventory, not sex and relationships.

"No. Never. I tried, Vince. I can't…" Trina's voice trailed off.

He was tempted to ask why, but it wasn't the gentlemanly thing to do. If there was one thing he knew about women, it was to give them space.

As Trina went on, she sounded more and more anxious with each word. "He hasn't asked me straight out. But what he does when we're alone, it's enough to tell me what he really wants. I know I'm supposed to like it. He's my boyfriend, after all. But I can't seem to get myself to give in."

He listened to her breathing for several long moments before he spoke, as gently and as patiently as he could. "Then don't give in, if you don't want to."

"Wouldn't that frustrate him, or make him angry? Turn him off?"

Vincent knew about frustration very well, but this was not about him. "If he really loves you and wants to marry you, he should damn well be willing to wait until you're ready."

"Would you wait, Vince?" Her voice was quiet. "If you were in his place?"

"You know me better than that. I would never even consider putting you in a predicament like this. That's not love, Trina. Not even close."

Damn it to hell.

This wasn't supposed to be about him. Not in the fucking least.

"I never thought of it that way," she said. "When James first became my boyfriend, I was so happy. Everyone kept telling me how lucky I was."

Not everyone, he wanted to correct her.

"He is so handsome and dreamy, you know? He is a famous model and all that. I thought I have to keep him happy, to keep him."

"Are you happy now?" That seemed to be the last word he could think of to describe her at the moment.

"To be honest, it's hard to be happy when your relationship is like a ticking time bomb. Lately, all I could think about is that it's only a matter of time before James asks. What if I can't give him what he wants? What if I make the wrong decision? What if he leaves me?"

It didn't sound like a healthy relationship. It sounded an awful lot like co-dependency.

"What if you think about what would make you happy, Trina?"

"Me? I don't know."

He couldn't blame her. Sometimes being in the safety of one's comfort zone mattered more than pursuing happiness. Sometimes the risk of getting out wasn't worth it, if it meant venturing into the unknown.

If it meant getting hurt.

"Once you figure it out, I get first dibs. I'll be here to listen. I might even splurge on some cookies. You know, those nasty sweet ones from Greenbelt you like so much."

He was rewarded by a small giggle. "Yeah, those."

"Think about what would make you happy, Trina, and make your decisions based on that. Not on what would make someone else happy, especially at your expense."

He hoped there was at least some clarity in her mind, or even a hint of a smile on her face.

"Thanks, VAT," she finally said. "You're the best, you know that?"

"Don't tell anyone, okay? My services are exclusive."

"To me?" He could hear the coyness, the humor, back in her voice. It was the best he could ask for, under the circumstances.

"Always have been."

"See you Monday, Vince. I'm really sorry if I bothered you on your weekend."

"It's okay. You can bother me anytime."

Trina thanked him again and hung up.

He stood up, plugged the phone into its charger, and sat back down on the couch. He picked up his mug for a sip. The coffee was now cold and flat, almost bitter.

He felt just as cold and flat as he thought of Abella, with her.

Trina.

He first met her six years ago, when she did his pre-interview at the firm. She was the most breathtaking woman he had ever laid eyes on, an opinion the years had not changed. She had smooth caramel skin, an hourglass figure, and long wavy hair a deep shade of mahogany. Her face had a sincere warmth he could just stare at and drink in for hours.

His first impression was that she was the human equivalent of the Energizer bunny, someone who kept going and going and barely stopped talking while at it.

Instead of finding her lively manner annoying, he found himself warming up, to the point of allowing her to christen him with a new nickname. It was little wonder she was the one usually assigned to potential hires or new employees.

It was a wonder, however, how they became friends. The first thing he could think of was how she could so easily get him to open up, or at least talk. Other people at the firm, even his fellow auditors, gave him space to work and move around the office without much need for social interaction. He had a reputation for no-frills efficiency, and he had to admit it commanded respect.

Trina did not give him the wide berth others did. She simply found her way into his life and settled in it, the same way she would barge into his office any time she wanted and sit in weird positions on the chairs facing his desk. Their friendship had lasted the better part of the past five years, to the point that his sister thought she was his girlfriend when Trina showed up at their aunt's funeral.

Now, he pondered the advice he had given her.

Think about what would make you happy.

Was he a hypocrite to give a confused woman this kind of advice, when he couldn't even apply it to his own life?

Then again, he wasn't the one in a relationship, not the one who faced the risk of a broken heart.

Or was he?

He knew from the moment Trina had started talking about things getting serious with Abella that his own heart was on the line. It was only a matter of time before it got ripped into shreds. He predicted it would either be at the sight of a ring on her finger or of the very woman herself in a wedding dress.

He was prepared for it, as long as she didn't know. He could face it, the same way he had faced everything his whole life.

Alone.

now and forever

Done, dusted and double ruled.

Vincent's words echoed in her mind as she lifted her chin and walked straight into the drizzling Manila night, ignoring the politely disguised yet obviously curious stares of the doorman and security guard stationed at the hotel's front entrance.

More like fully depreciated and written off.

She was a fool to think there would be at least some sort of compromise, that James would give her room to think about what she really wanted.

Instead, he had wined and dined her, then went in for the kill.

It shouldn't have surprised her.

The rain was the first one that month, adding insult to her already dreary state of affairs. The typhoon season was still months away, but, hell, anything goes.

Life seemed to be trying to throw as much crap as it could at her, all at the same time.

The hotel was located in the Bay Area, close to the metropolitan but posh and exclusive enough to merit its high profile and ludicrously expensive status.

There should be a few taxis around, in theory, but everyone drove their shiny, showy cars to and from this place, as far as she could see.

She was the only one walking.

She could wait inside for a taxi, but she had more pride than that. No way in hell was she staying.

Trina clutched her leather handbag tightly, debating whether or not to use it as some kind of umbrella, finally dismissing the idea as pointless.

Her little black dress and matching suede shoes had already gone to waste. She wished she had not splurged as much during her shopping trip that afternoon, in an effort to keep her mind off the conversation with Vincent and the inevitable with James.

The downpour had increased in intensity by the time she reached the main gates of the hotel. Half-blinded by rain water, she continued to plod onwards.

"I met someone else, Trina."

Those five words tolled at the back of her head like some kind of death knell.

James had gone on and on with his explanation. Perhaps he'd thought it would make her feel better, if there was a clear reason for their break-up.

"I thought you loved me, but I never felt it. She made me feel loved, in ways more than words could ever explain."

Feel it, my ass, she thought bitterly.

"I tried to make our relationship work but nothing ever seemed to get through to you. I hope you'll understand where I'm coming from. I've fallen in love with her."

The funny part was that she understood very clearly, maybe a little too well for her own good.

The moment her now-ex-boyfriend had finished his

confession, she had stood up, with as much dignity as she could muster, and made the most regal exit she could from the restaurant.

She took pride in two things: First, she'd kept her head held high; second, she'd never cried.

She had no desire to cry. If anything, she could almost describe her feelings, after the initial hurtful blow of rejection to her ego, as a combination of relief and lightness, as if she'd just been unburdened of something ridiculously heavy.

"Think about what would make you happy, Trina."

She would give anything right now, if she could just talk to Vincent.

Anything to hear his voice, always a source of comfort and reason.

As soon as she got home, she'd try and give him a call…

A sudden, deafening screech cut through the fog of her thoughts.

She momentarily forgot her troubles as she, dazed and confused, faced the direction of the high-pitched sound.

A black car, with prism-like headlights, had stopped a few feet away from her. She stared as the car's wipers moved furiously, rhythmically, across the windshield.

She had not seen any cars coming her way. There was no one else outside, no one else on the road. Not in this weather.

She was alone, wasn't she?

A man, dressed all in the same color as the dark vehicle before her, stepped out of the car.

His clothing was shiny, like leather. With his hair styled

into spikes, he looked like a sleek nocturnal animal, or maybe the lead singer of a rock band.

"Trina? What the fuck are you doing here?"

The voice was very familiar, but the sight wasn't. The rain and the headlights danced around her like strobes in a disco, making her dizzy.

She had to make sense of this.

So she uttered his name, in both uncertainty and unabashed curiosity.

"Vincent?"

The man who sounded but barely looked like Vincent Tugade sloshed his way to her side, his eyes glittering even in the cover of night.

"Have you lost your mind, Trina? You shouldn't be out on the road like this."

"Vincent?" she repeated the name, not quite sure if she wanted to be right or wrong. "What are you doing here? Why do you look like that?"

"We have to get you off the streets." He held out a hand to her. "Come on."

She could only stare at him. The dinner, the near-accident, now this man. It was too much.

"Get in the car, Trina, please."

She backed away. She didn't have the energy to put up with more surprises tonight. "Just go, okay? Leave me alone."

"What are you doing?" He stepped closer and took hold of her arm. "I'm taking you home, okay? Please get in the car and we can talk about it."

He gave her that familiar indulgent smile, none too sincerely this time. She recognized him like this, vaguely.

"I don't think—"

Before she could continue, he had his hand on the small of her back and was guiding her to the car. Too weary to put up a fight, she allowed herself to be pushed, albeit gently, into the front seat.

He silently got into the driver's side. In the dim light, she could see his lips set in a firm line. He took off his jacket and gave it to her. He was dressed in a black sleeveless shirt underneath.

"Stay warm. I'll turn off the air conditioner."

"Thanks," she heard herself say.

"You're welcome."

He reached for the dashboard and started adjusting buttons and switches. His arms had well-defined muscles and an assortment of tattoos going all the way down to his forearms.

To stop herself from staring at him so rudely, Trina gave the jacket a shake and put it around her shoulders. She could feel her new dress soak water into the car seat. She buckled up when she saw him do the same. She clutched her bag and the seatbelt close to her as she looked out of the window at the rainy night.

The car hummed to life and started to cruise forward.

"Vince, I…" It took a while before she could work up the energy and courage to look at the almost-stranger next to her, much less talk to him.

"I'm sorry," she completed lamely, clenching her hands, feeling them shake with the residual cold.

He was quiet for several seconds. "For what?"

"For all the trouble. One thing after another went downhill. Before I knew it, I was out of there like my ass was on fire."

He shook his head, but kept his eyes trained on the road. "In a way, it's a good thing I was the one you ran into. The car's brakes hold up pretty well even when they're wet."

The thought of brakes was enough to make her feel even colder. Had it been another car, or another driver, she wasn't quite sure where she would be now.

In hindsight, she should have stayed inside the hotel and waited for a taxi, or got James to drop her home, not wandered out into the rain like some tragic heroine in a cheap romance novel. The only real tragedy of the entire evening was the sorry shape of her pricey new dress and its matching shoes.

"Still, this entire drama is my fault," she admitted.

"Drama?"

"The walk-out, the emoting in the rain, the getting nearly ran over part. I guess I was too proud to put up with any more bullshit."

"I see." Vincent held on to the steering wheel with one hand, his other hand going up to rub out droplets of water stuck to his spiky hair. "I'm sure that wasn't how you had the night planned out, was it?"

"Well, no." She gave her eyes a little rub, still unable to

reconcile the fact that this tattooed, leather-clad man was the Vincent she had known all these years. She didn't even know he had arms like that.

For the first time, she noted that this wasn't his Toyota sedan, but something else entirely.

The black car had metal panels on the sides, a convex roof and a windshield lined with what looked like steel reinforcements. The seats were wrapped in dark leather that matched his clothes. All over the interior, there were stickers and buttons with death motifs, such as skulls, chains and spikes. The buttons and gauges on the dashboard before her looked like the control panel of a mad scientist.

His voice was calm and measured as he spoke. "If I had known you were going to be at the hotel, I would have picked you up. You should have called me."

"I dragged you through the pathetic story of my relationship this morning. I could never do that to you twice. Besides, I never thought you would be here, at this time. Like that." She gestured to all of him in general.

"Like what?" He glanced at her, tilting his head curiously.

"Like, different. Dangerous. You know, someone capable of running James over."

To her surprise, he smiled. "Whoever said I wasn't? All you have to do is ask."

She sighed. "That sounds very tempting right now."

His next words were so serious it was hard to discern whether or not he really meant them. "If you really want to do a number on Abella, we can turn back and get him. The track near the bay will be closed by now, but I'm sure I could get us in. I've raced there since they started building it, right after the mall opened."

Race.

VAT was a racer. Suddenly, the car, the clothes and the skulls all made sense.

"Thanks for the generous and potentially criminal offer, but I'll pass." She could feel the beginnings of a small smile on her lips.

They didn't talk for a while as he deftly wove the car through the Saturday night traffic of the city, taking shortcuts through tiny side streets. By the time they were out of the Bay Area, she felt calm enough to loosen her grip on her bag and the seatbelt and settle more comfortably in the front seat.

"You still live at the tower?"

"Yes. I'm surprised you remember."

He shrugged. "We should be there soon. I know a shortcut near the hospital. That should keep us away from most of the late night traffic."

"You're the best, VAT," she said, echoing her sentiments from earlier that day. "Thanks for putting up with my crap."

He didn't answer, but a little while later she felt his hand on her shoulder.

"It's not crap. I'm very sorry this happened." He gave a gentle squeeze before letting go. "You deserve to be happy."

She tugged at his jacket, pulling it more snugly around her. She never knew leather could feel so soft.

"At least James had the guts to call it off himself. I suppose he needed something I couldn't give. We both wanted different things. I stressed all about it for nothing."

Vincent shook his head. "Not nothing. I'm sure whatever you two had, it meant more to you than it did to him."

Trina looked out the window again. She could barely see a thing, except for torrents of water, thick mist, and flickering lights.

It was a fitting metaphor for what she had with James. What she thought she had with him. She never really saw what it was, just blurry lines and splashes of color. Everything she made out of it was her own interpretation, not the truth.

Her newly-ended relationship was a joke, if not a failure, from the very start. Marrying her was something James had never even remotely considered. She knew that now.

"James told me he met someone else while on a job in Bali months back. It doesn't take a genius to figure out he got what he wanted from her. Apparently they kept in touch after that."

The memory of her ex's confession was still fresh in her mind, spilling out easily. Trina couldn't even remember the other girl's name. "James said she was far less…I don't know, frigid than I am, I suppose. The exact words he used were 'cold' and 'walled off.'"

"Sounds like he thinks you're some kind of high security vault. One he doesn't have the access code to, the poor bastard."

"I never thought you'd ever feel sorry for him." She gave him a sidelong glance. "You hate his guts."

"Am I that obvious?"

"Kind of, especially as you offered to run him over if I wanted you to."

"That prick doesn't know what he's missing out on," he declared solemnly, in a tone that begged no argument.

Minutes later, they pulled up in front of a high-rise condominium complex. He parked in an open spot on the sidewalk, got out of the car, and opened the passenger door for her.

She shakily stepped out, her wet shoes digging into her skin as she walked carefully on the rain-drenched pavement. Her dress had dried partially, but it still clung to her body like a second skin. To her surprise, she felt self-conscious under the bright fluorescent lights of the building's main entrance as he followed her to the foyer.

"Thank you, Vince." She pulled his jacket off her shoulders and handed it back to him. "For everything."

"You're welcome." He reached out and took the jacket back. "Will you be okay? Can I get you anything, from the pharmacy or somewhere?"

"No, I'm fine. Thanks for the offer." No matter how he dressed, he was always reliable.

Tonight, he just appeared a little more exciting than usual.

It occurred to her how different it had felt to look at her ex-boyfriend's mestizo, camera-ready face, compared to the darker, harder countenance of the man before her.

With Vincent, she had always been at ease. She never

had to second-guess herself or question her own actions and decisions.

His words in the car rattled around the back of her mind.

That prick doesn't know what he's missing out on.

What if she asked herself that question?

What am I missing out on?

He was looking straight back at her. She had no idea what was in his head. She never really had. She'd always expected him, by default, to come through, listen, accept, and give—cookies, advice, time, his presence. He even came through for her at this time, without her asking, without him knowing, by sheer chance of fate.

Why did he?

Trina didn't know if she felt guilty, confused or overwhelmed. Perhaps all three. Seeing Vincent in a different light, in the rainy cold of reality, was unnerving.

She needed to put this entire weekend behind her, as soon as possible.

He stepped closer and wrapped one arm around her shoulders. He gave her a quick peck on the cheek; it felt familiar, yet, in her waterlogged state, she felt a little breathless at the contact. She could feel blood rushing to her head.

"Rest up, Trina," he said as he pulled away. "Call me tomorrow if you need anything, okay?"

She didn't let him pull away completely. Instead, she put her hands on his tattooed forearms. Still halfway in his embrace, she could see that his eyes were almost silver in color, not the greyish-brown she thought they were.

"Would you like to come up for some coffee?" Her own voice sounded higher-pitched, even shrill, to her own ears. She had no idea where it came from, but it was all her.

He hesitated. He was still predictable enough, but she had always liked that about him. She knew his answer before he said it, but she didn't quite anticipate the tension she felt emanating from his body.

"Sure."

❧

What the fuck are you doing, Tugade?

Vincent mentally confronted himself as he followed her off the elevator. They had reached the seventh floor of her apartment building.

"My place is this way." Trina was a few steps ahead. He could see she was limping a little and dragging her feet. He thought of helping her, but the idea of touching her again didn't sound very smart at the moment.

He shouldn't have touched her like he had downstairs. They had always hugged and kissed each other chastely, but, tonight, it felt very different. For starters, she kept giving him wide-eyed looks, from all directions, as if she was seeing him for the first time.

Vince knew those kinds of looks. He had given her those before, many times over, when he was certain she couldn't see him. He had never stopped, not since he first saw her when she came out to the firm's lobby for his pre-interview.

He knew his feelings for her very well, had grappled with

and successfully kept them buried under a platonic veneer. Trina, on the other, had no idea. If she did, she would probably be out of his life like her 'ass was on fire.'

It was a risk he could not take. He had too much to lose. Her friendship, her trust, and, above all, *her*.

Katrina David was someone he could never afford to lose.

With her freshly single from a break-up, this was the worst possible time to even consider that he had a chance. He would rather have himself run over on the track by the other racers.

Trina stopped at a unit numbered 704. "Home sweet home. Can you help me, Vince?"

He had to snap himself out of any delusional episode he had going. She was holding out her keys.

"The gold one, please."

He took the bunch rather abruptly from her grasp and moved closer to the door. As he bent over to unlock it, he felt Trina wrap her arms around his left arm as she leaned against him. Up close, he could see her wet dress hugging every curve of her body. Her cleavage was practically next to his face as she shifted her weight from foot to foot.

"I'm so tired, Vince," she said. "I think I spent next month's salary shopping this afternoon for an outfit that I completely ruined."

Ruined? That was the last thing on his mind, looking at her in the little black dress.

He averted his eyes and thanked all existing higher

powers when he heard the lock give way. He was too close for comfort. He would have that coffee and get himself the fuck home.

She did not let him go as they went in, clinging to his arm as she hobbled into the apartment and pointed out the light switches. He gave in to his earlier gentlemanly inclination and led her to the white couch in the middle of her living room. She heaved herself gratefully onto the seat and took off her shoes.

"Major ouch." She shook her head and made clucking sounds as she started flexing her toes and rotating her ankles.

He took the opportunity to step away from her. He could leave. She was fine. He had made sure of that.

"I think I'll call it a night," he said. "I'd better go."

True to form, Trina hopped back to her bare feet. "What are you talking about? Sit down. Let me get you that coffee. It's premium roasted Arabica. I'll even give you the rest of the beans, too."

He swallowed hard and seated himself hesitantly on the couch, next to the spot she had just vacated. He tossed his jacket to a nearby plastic chair. "I'm sorry about the wet clothes."

"I did the same thing to your car. Call it even between us."

He watched her disappear behind a curtained doorway. He looked around. The place was neat and orderly; the colors were a mishmash of white, brown, orange and yellow. Even on a rainy night, the place looked bright and alive.

Minutes later, he saw her head poke through the curtains. "Vince? Come join me in the kitchen. I put on some croissants, too."

"That would be great." He stood up and followed her into the next room. It was fairly compact, cozy, outfitted with sunny yellow tiles. Next to a small glass window overlooking the city, there was a wooden table with matching seats for three.

She gestured for him to sit on one of the chairs. She was quiet as she poured them both coffee. She placed a plate full of croissants between them and sat from across him.

"Thanks for looking out for me tonight. Goodness knows I have no business troubling you for anything. I honestly thought this morning was the end of it."

He took a sip of the coffee. It was strong and scalding hot. "Is that how you think of yourself, Trina? Trouble?"

He watched her take a sip of coffee, twitching a little uncomfortably in her damp dress as she thought about his question. He wondered if it would be appropriate if he suggested she change clothes, more for his state of mind than her own health and comfort.

"It seems I could never give anyone what they want from me," she declared thoughtfully. "I don't know if that's trouble or not."

"It's called making your choices, I believe. Definitely not trouble."

Trina shrugged. "Is it? James thinks I'm a cold bitch. My friends think I'm so flighty I couldn't even commit to their vacation plans. My own family thinks I'm all talk and no substance, that's why I haven't been promoted to HR Manager."

The rapid-fire honesty in her declaration was a heart-rending surprise. He was sorely tempted to close the distance between them and take her into his arms.

Instead, he took another sip of coffee. "Do you agree with any of them?"

She shook her head. "I love my job and I like people. I actually enjoy my work. If I were manager, I would have to spend the whole damn day writing reports, signing stupid forms, and talking to higher management. As for trips, I don't really want to go on a lot of them because traveling's so expensive and I want to pay off this unit as soon as possible."

Her down-to-earth practicality was something he admired immensely. "Can't argue with the numbers on that one."

"I know, right?" Her shoulders heaved in a sigh. "And James…well, tonight pretty much sums it all up. For the record, he broke it off, but I was the one who walked out first."

"There you go. You've made your choices. If people don't appreciate that, it's their problem, not yours."

She smiled at him for what seemed the first time that evening. "I think you're right."

"You should start thinking about what you want, rather than what other people want and expect from you. As I said, you deserve to be happy. Do what makes you happy."

If only he could do the same thing. If only he had the balls to follow his own advice.

Her smile brightened a little more. "This makes me happy. Having you here."

It felt as if she had stabbed him, front and center. To disguise the tightness in his chest, he affected a grin and lifted his coffee mug in a toast. "To your happiness, Trina."

She leaned forward, wrapping her hands around her mug. Her eyes narrowed, focusing on him like laser beams, as if she was trying to read his thoughts.

"Why do you do this, Vince?"

"Do what?"

"This. You look after me. Without asking for anything in return."

He swallowed the bite of croissant in his mouth. "We're friends. That's what friends do."

"I don't really know anything about you, do I? I mean, you've never even told me you had a car like that, or you race…I don't even know if you have a girl waiting for you somewhere and, somehow, tonight her man's babysitting me instead. That kind of thing."

He had to smile at her words. She always gave him more credit than he deserved, especially with women. "You know there is no girl. There's no one. As for racing, it's something you don't exactly advertise when you work in a Big Four firm."

"Will you take me to a race next time?"

"I'll take you, just promise you won't tell anyone in the office. With that dress, you'll fit right in."

"This outfit has not been a total waste, then."

"No, not at all." After a quick glance at his watch, he got to his feet. All that talk about his personal life and the absence of romance from it was making him uncomfortable. She would prod and pry all the time, but when she suggested becoming part of it, even in a race, it made him feel exposed, vulnerable. "It's late, Trina. I'd better go."

She nodded and got up, too, following him back to her colorful living room. She handed over his jacket and a paper bag. "The coffee, as promised. If you do decide to bring it to work on Monday, save some for me."

"Not a chance," he said, grinning down at her.

Instead of responding by whacking him on the arm or giving one of her usual silly faces, Trina stared at him with wide, almost doe-like, eyes. She put her arms around his shoulders and invaded what little personal space there was left between them, never taking her gaze off him.

"Trina?" he asked, hesitantly, trapped but not exactly unwilling. "What are you doing?"

"What makes me happy."

With her fingers in his hair, she brought his head down for a kiss.

She heard his sharp intake of breath, felt a sudden tautness take over his body. Something fell to the floor, crunching under their feet. The world around them began to spin as she pushed her body against his.

This was something she had never wanted to do with James.

With Vincent, it was the exact opposite. The moment he gave her that big smile, there was nothing more she wanted in the world than to get all that leather off him and have him for herself

She didn't want him to go.

The desire she felt was as clear as the sky on a bright, sunny day. There was neither confusion nor uncertainty. There was only the feeling she was exactly where she was meant to be, with the person she was meant to be with.

His arms, wonderfully warm through her damp clothes, went around her as he started to kiss her back, slowly at first, then with more urgency. He tasted of coffee and rain, of salt and a hint of sugar. She couldn't get enough of it.

Kissing alone wouldn't satisfy her. She had never been more certain of something, ever. Her hands took a life of their own, moving beneath his shirt, until she could feel the hardness of his torso under her fingertips.

He didn't keep idle. He nipped at her earlobes and neck as he began to push the straps of the black dress off her shoulders, baring a wider path for his lips to trace.

She moaned when his mouth found its way to her collarbone. She dug her fingers into his back as he devoured the sensitive skin of her throat and chest.

She found her voice and, for what seemed like the very first time, the words to tell him what she truly wanted.

"Please don't go. Don't leave me alone tonight."

He didn't answer but instead swept her off the floor and laid her down on the couch, covering her body with his. When he finally spoke, it was against her lips.

"No one is leaving tonight, Trina, as long as you tell me this is what you really want."

Oh, god. She could tell what *he* wanted, felt it through those tight black pants that seemed molded to his long legs, as they resumed their heated kissing. Her own body responded as she shifted her hips closer, higher.

She put her hands on his cheeks and stared into his eyes, unable to stop herself from drowning in them. He was fascinating and so deliciously male. Why did she have to look at other men when she had him in front of her the whole time?

"This is what I've always wanted," she whispered. "I'm very sure."

His lips found hers again. His tongue delved into her mouth as his hands found their way through her clothing. He easily slid the dress off her, followed by her black lace bra and thong.

She had dressed for someone she had never desired, only to be undressed by the one man she had wanted—needed—all this time.

It was worth it, after all, she thought, as she felt him touch that intimate, soaking spot between her legs, felt his mouth close around each of her nipples in turn before making its way down to her heat. She squealed when she felt his tongue on her, her hips bucking wildly. She reached out for him, fumbling with his belt, only to growl and command him to take his clothes off, too.

When he stood bare before her, she marveled at the sheer sight of him. Without clothes, he was more muscle-bound than she'd ever imagined. His tattoos wound around his upper body like chains.

She held out her arms and he went into them. He was very gentle, his voice soft in her ear, promising he would never hurt her. His fingers coaxed her to open, drawing out her pleasure and her need. His lips were on her mouth, on her hair, on her neck, as she ground herself against him, knowing exactly what her body was reaching for.

His timing was exquisite. She felt herself stretch as he entered and sheathed himself inside her. She was the first to move, her hands going up into his hair, her arms locking around his upper back, her teeth grazing his shoulder.

He matched her movements as if they were in a perfectly choreographed dance, his hands on her hips and legs, guiding her body to meet and move against his. He was good, so good.

She felt it then, a warm, snaking sensation beginning to build inside her very core, wrapping itself around her, until she felt it explode between them and send shockwaves of pleasure throughout her body. She heard herself moan his name, followed by incoherent mewls and loud gasps.

"I can't hold back," he whispered hoarsely, before she felt him tense up and move faster, harder, deeper into her. He made a throaty, guttural sound as his body convulsed on top of hers. She watched pleasure cross his features, savoring how tightly he held on to her, as if for dear life.

She put her arms around him as he slumped on top of her, burying his head between her breasts. She closed her eyes, basking in the bliss that still hummed throughout her body, and the familiar scent and warmth of the man she now had in her arms.

"Vince?" she said into his rumpled hair.

"Yeah?" His eyes were half-closed, his nose nuzzling one breast.

"I'm glad it's you. I've always wanted it to be you."

When she was rewarded by that grin again, and the glitter of what she now recognized as desire in his eyes, she knew they were both in for a long, sleepless night.

This time, not alone.

The first thing he realized, when he woke up, was that he wasn't alone in bed.

Vincent found himself looking at long locks of mahogany hair spread out before him. They belonged to the woman sleeping next to him, spooned naked against his body. He still had one arm around her. Her bare buttocks were pressed against his leg.

He slowly reached over to push the hair away from her face. Trina looked beautifully content in sleep. In the morning light, he could see that her pink lips looked slightly swollen.

Morning light.

There was a small digital clock on the nightstand. It read 9:43.

He had overslept by almost five hours, in a bed that wasn't his.

This bed had sheets and pillowcases in white, orange and pink. A peach-colored teddy bear glared at him from its perch next to the digital clock.

So much for his routine.

But this was the kind of Saturday night and Sunday morning he could get used to.

They had made love all over her apartment, and moved to her bedroom afterwards. After savoring all of her, he decided she tasted like mocha, strong and addictive, with an undeniable hint of sweetness.

The last thing he could recall was Trina grinding on top of him, before he turned her over and took her from behind, tantalized by the perfect roundness of her butt the entire time. At some point, they fell asleep, the rain stopped, and the sun rose, in no particular order.

"Good morning." Her voice was sweet, shy, almost girlish. Her eyes were half-open, still a little clouded with sleep.

"Good morning, baby girl," he said, trying out the endearment for the first time in his life. It sounded right. It felt good to say it.

She turned to face him, her arms going around his neck with surprising familiarity. She kissed him square on the lips. "How'd you sleep?"

"Very good. I just woke up, too. I was watching you."

She blushed and buried her face in his neck. "Don't do that."

"Do what?"

"That thing with your eyes."

He had no idea what she was talking about. "Something wrong with my eyes?"

"No. Yes. Whenever you look at me like that, that's it. I'm gone." Understanding slowly dawned on him, as she began nibbling at his neck.

"Trina?" he prompted, tenderly, reaching for her chin.

"Yes?" She settled against the crook of his arm, as comfortably as she would sit in his office.

"What happens to us now?"

She looked at him with surprise in her eyes but said nothing.

He swallowed. He might as well get it over with, before nerves got the better of him.

"Would you like to be my girlfriend? I suppose, sooner rather than later, I would have to propose, too, seeing that we didn't use—"

She began to giggle, and then laughed, so merrily and contagiously he forgot any apprehensions he had. She wriggled closer to him.

"To all of the above, my answer is yes."

His response was to kiss her soundly.

She wasn't finished. "My only condition is that you've got to have the energy for this, Mr. Tugade. I don't want to have fun all by myself."

He raised himself up by the elbow and arranged his demeanor into what she called his Presentation Mode.

"Miss David, allow me to show you the real definition of energy. I hope you're ready for a demonstration."

With her laughter washing over him, he plunged into her waiting arms.

THREE

Axis

"You. Insult. Me."

Koreen Cisco punctuated each word deliberately as she lowered her hips to the practice mat and deftly maneuvered Royce Duran overhead.

He barely had enough time to brace his stomach and get into a quick forward roll, landing none too gracefully in a supine position. It was a miracle he made it without breaking his neck.

"I. Actually. Felt. That." He cringed as pain shot through his lower back, feeling his age now more than ever. Dimly, he was aware of other people in the gym who had momentarily paused in whatever they were doing to look their way.

"No less than you deserve," Koreen snapped back. "The

next time you walk in here to challenge the sensei, you had better come prepared."

She was grinning from ear to ear as she looked down at him. Royce watched her half in amusement, half in amazement.

Koreen barely cleared five feet. She had black hair that sported an uneven bob cut, skin with an unusual reddish-gold tone, and the strength to break his neck with probably just a flick of her tiny wrist.

It was her chocolate-brown eyes, however, that made her different from everyone else. She had cat's eyes, which could practically wound with a glance. He figured she was very capable of actually doing that, if she set her mind to it.

"I never imagined you would ever look as miserable as you do right now. You have always been my best sparring opponent, Duran. What happened to all those lightning takedowns?"

Royce smiled inwardly. Leave it to Koreen to gloat whenever she had the upper hand. The competitive relationship he shared with her was as natural to him as the sun rising in the morning. All through elementary and secondary school, they had been pitted against each other academically to the point of sharing the valedictory honors at graduation. During high school, they both took up Judo and sparred against each other regularly.

Things changed when they reached college. Royce moved to the capital to join the elite Integrated Arts and Medicine program of the country's premier state university.

Koreen stayed in town to continue her studies and now taught Mathematics in the same high school they had both attended. She also became a part-time Judo instructor at their old martial arts gymnasium.

Ever the overachieving whiz kid, he had thought wryly, upon hearing about all the things she had been up to.

Royce had, admittedly, been pathetically lacking in keeping up with his training. There were barely any Judo schools in the part of Saudi Arabia where his company was based. Karate, Taekwondo and Brazilian Jiu-jitsu were undoubtedly more popular. Besides, he would actually be lucky if he had any time left to train. He had worked for the Saudi-based transcription company the last seven years, five as the General Manager. Reporting only to the Saudi prince who owned the business, Royce had set up branches in Dubai and Pune over the years, with the Philippines as the next frontier. To date, he nearly had a thousand people in his employ.

"Well." he replied, smiling and taking the hand she extended to help himself up, "maybe all those years behind a desk has made me soft." His smile became devilish. "Or maybe not."

Before her brain could register what was going on, Koreen found herself pinned to the mat, ballroom-dip style. His left hand was around her waist, the other braced on the surface to keep both their balance. She realized that Royce did so to spare her own back from the impact.

He had just waltzed back into the gym that very afternoon. He had done enough showing-off to last her a lifetime.

Royce Duran. Ever since they were children, he was a paragon of everything she had secretly envied. He was good-looking, effortlessly athletic, undeniably charismatic, and a natural-born leader. She relied on her smarts and the unusual amount of physical strength she was gifted with; she was a far cry from being described as an attractive girl. Competing with someone whom other people always seemed to like more had been exhausting.

His smooth brown face was very, very close to hers. Koreen felt his almost-black irises look right into her soul. The scent of him engulfed her. It was a sporty kind of cologne, understated and subtle.

Their eyes locked.

Then Royce said: "Or maybe I just got lucky." This time, he effortlessly pulled her to her feet. "You haven't lost your touch, Koreen."

She felt the breath that she had been holding exit her lungs in a loud *whoosh*.

"You're not that bad," she said grudgingly. "Not yet, anyway."

"I should be grateful for that, I guess," he replied, as they faced each other and bowed. "Given how rusty I have apparently become."

"You should be on your way before I catch my second wind." Koreen averted her attention from him and gestured for her students to take their spots on the training mats. She was positive she heard giggles and snickers. It was, after all, a milestone to see the teacher get whipped in the ass.

"As you wish, Sensei." He bowed again and paused when she was at eye level. "I'll pick you up from school Friday afternoon. Dinner's on me, of course. The winner always picks up the tab." Royce straightened and headed for the men's locker room.

"Not on your life, Duran," she whispered, glaring at his retreating back and smoothing down the wrinkles of her white kimono.

"Ten rounds of running around the gym to warm up," she snapped at her students. Where was their loyalty to their sensei when she needed it most?

She only felt satisfied when she heard groans and protests instead.

"Excuse me, Miss Cisco?"

Koreen looked up from the stack of test papers she was grading. It was late afternoon. All the other teachers had left for the day. She was savoring a rare moment of solitude in the faculty room before going to the gym later that evening for a grueling two-hour session with her advanced class.

One of her senior students in Advanced Algebra had poked his head through the half-open doorway. He was wearing a school sports jersey, probably still at practice in the courts near her office. "Yes, Paul? How can I help you?"

"There's someone asking for you. He said he was a classmate of yours."

"He's here?" The words escaped her mouth before she could stop herself. She had completely forgotten about Royce's dinner offer.

"Hey, Paul. Is your Ma'am Cisco in there?" She heard a deeper, older male voice coming from the corridor.

Paul's head disappeared from sight. "Yup," she heard the boy say. "She's right in there, Mister Duran."

A few more words were exchanged, before she heard a set of receding footsteps.

"Good afternoon, Ma'am." It was Royce's turn to poke his head through the doorway. "Although you look more like a student, I'm getting a very strange sense of *déjà vu* right now."

Koreen glared at him "Did you come all the way here just to throw jabs at my age?"

"Actually, I came here to make good on my dinner invitation," he answered, deadpan.

"I thought you were joking." Koreen sighed and shook her head. "I honestly didn't think you meant any of it."

Royce held up his hands in what looked like mock surrender.

It was then she saw that he actually came *dressed* for dinner. His hair was gelled neatly and he was wearing a well-cut aqua-colored polo shirt and dark blue slacks. His feet were encased in what looked like black leather boots, shiny and expensive looking. He was not conventionally handsome with his sharp features, but her eyes were irresistibly drawn to his face. Laugh lines and other signs of maturity now tempered his boyish toughness, but she would be a hypocrite if she denied how attractive he really was.

"I meant what I said," he replied, with a charming grin. "I'm sorry if you thought I was trying to pull some kind of stunt on you. At our age, we should have already outgrown whatever bad blood we had between us by now."

Koreen put down her pen and pushed the papers on her desk to one side. This was not the kind of exchange she'd expected.

"It's not bad blood. It's just that you have a gift of getting on my nerves. You were always in my way, Duran. I put up with it for more than ten years when we were kids."

The easy, lighthearted cast to his face disappeared at her words, changing to a more deflated look. "It was never my intention to get in your way or on your nerves. I was just trying to be friendly."

They had been rivals, competitors, sparring partners. Never friends.

There had always been a line between them, an invisible axis, that bisected the world. One could never share with the other.

"You came back home like some kind of conquering hero," she declared, rising to her feet. Sitting behind the desk felt suffocating all of a sudden. She made her way around and sat at the edge of her table, biding her time to organize her thoughts. "Everyone in town has been talking about your Transcription Tower, how many jobs it would create, how a son of Iloilo never forgot his roots while he was making waves in the BPO industry. What was I supposed to think when you walked into the gym four days ago?"

"That I suck at Judo now?" he offered.

"That you came to gloat." Somehow, she felt defeated, drained, as soon as she said it.

"Gloat?" Royce walked further into the faculty room. His presence seemed to dwarf everything else in sight. He stopped a few feet in front of her. "That was the last thing on my mind, Koreen. Why would I gloat about anything, especially to you, of all people?"

She averted her eyes from his. *To make me feel as inconsequential as you always have.* She wanted to say it, so badly, but stopped herself. Instead, she listened to her own intakes of breath, to him breathing a short distance away. She could have sworn she could hear his heart pounding, or maybe it was her own. She wasn't sure of anything at that point.

"Koreen," he finally said. "Please look at me."

She did, not without hesitation. His dark eyes were laser-focused and unblinking against her own. "What?"

"I wanted to see you. When I found out you were still in town, I thought right away you would be the best person to run the Transcription Tower. I wanted to offer you a stake in the business."

This, she thought dazedly. This was the last thing she had ever expected him to say.

By far, it was the biggest possible shock he could have

sprung on her. So much so, that all she could do was stare at him, dumbstruck.

"What made you think that?" she asked finally, carefully. "After all this time, you thought of me?"

He shrugged. "If I had to choose someone to trust my dreams and lifeblood with, it would be the smartest, hardest working and scariest person I know. You."

She had to shake her head. "You're crazy."

"There's no one like you, Koreen. Let me make that very clear. This is why I wanted to offer you partnership in our venture. I was going to tell you tonight, over dinner, under circumstances better than this."

For the longest time, and she could never really fathom how long, they both stood in the middle of the faculty room, wordlessly sizing each other up.

So this is how it feels to have your world turned upside down.

"I need some time to think about it," she heard herself say, after what seemed like the longest pause. "If that's what you're really asking."

"Yes, it is. Take all the time you need. I will arrange for the operations team in HQ to send you whatever you wish to know."

"Great." It was her turn to approach him. They were almost toe to toe when she stopped and looked him straight in the eye. "I have a class until nine o'clock tonight. What about dinner after?"

He was not the only one who could spring surprises.

The grin was back on his face in no time. "Dinner after."

The sedan he borrowed from his father pulled up the curb at exactly nine in the evening. From behind the wheel, Royce looked at the flight of stairs leading up to the gymnasium. Koreen's class was probably just wrapping up. He could wait.

It was strange, how quickly things could change. His seven years in Saudi Arabia had been a blur of endless work, fueled by a deep-rooted determination to bring a dream to life. The prince had repeatedly asked him to take a break: be with his family in the Philippines, find a wife, or simply take his mother and father on vacation. None of these mattered very much when Royce had his eyes on a goal.

Jeddah, Dubai, Pune, finally Iloilo. *Home,* where he was going to build a state-of-the-art transcription facility, possibly the biggest in Southeast Asia, and employ hundreds of his own countrymen.

Royce had come full circle.

It felt like he was back at the beginning, in some ways. A time in his life when all he wanted to do was impress the girl with the cat-like eyes. No matter what he did back then, she had always come out the smarter one in school, the one better prepared in projects and competitions, the one who could execute advanced Judo moves with the quiet strength and deadly precision of a born master.

Who could blame a man for trying then, and for trying again now?

When he found out she was still single, it was all he

could do to stop himself from kissing and doing other things to her in the middle of their old Judo gym, when he first saw her. Besides, if he'd tried anything, he would have been in the hospital right now, if he was lucky.

For now, he took comfort and assurance that he had made his offer clear and, at the same time, stopped pissing her off so much by making her understand how he actually thought of her.

As far as back as he could remember, he had always held Koreen Cisco in the highest regard. Hell, he would build a pedestal for her, if she asked nicely, or maybe twisted his arm a little bit. It wouldn't take much.

"Ouch." The woman he couldn't stop thinking about materialized from the semi-darkness outside the car, pulling open the passenger door and unceremoniously sliding into the seat beside him. "The hips are hurting, and they never lie. Remind me, Duran, how are old are we?"

"Thirty-two."

"Numbers could hurt so much," she declared, lowering a large purple backpack to the car floor next to her feet. "That's something they don't put in the math textbooks."

"Good evening to you, too, Sensei." He could not help but admire how good she looked in the tie-dyed shift she was wearing. It was green and brown, setting off her red-gold skin tone perfectly. The yellow-orange light of the car interior gave her a luminous aura.

"I'm sorry to have kept you waiting," she said, turning her full attention to him. He noticed that she had put on makeup, making her unforgettable eyes look even more feline than they already were. "I didn't want to look like a sack of charcoal. A judo-gi could only get me so far."

"You look beautiful," he said. Unable to resist, he leaned over and gave her a peck on the cheek. "Thanks for accepting my invitation."

He braced himself for her reaction. A well-placed slap across the face or a punch in the gut, perhaps. He was willing to sacrifice a few teeth or have a few ribs broken.

Instead, she put a hand on his shoulder, just as he was pulling away from her, effectively stopping him.

"You're welcome," she replied, before pulling him back in.

This time it was her turn to press her lips to his cheek, her mouth lingering for several long, sweet seconds.

She reached for the spot she had just kissed, her fingers slowly dragging over his skin. It took a few seconds for him to realize she was removing traces of her lipstick.

"I'm starving, Duran. Let's go."

She sipped the last few drops of her coffee, taking in the sight of him seated across from her at the table. All evening long, Royce had been relaxed and attentive, and so effortlessly funny. She had never really seen him that way before. Then again, she had never really spent any time with him in the past.

"I've never eaten so much in years," she said. "Thanks again."

He shook his head. "I had an ulterior motive, as I said earlier. But you're welcome. I'm glad we didn't have to talk business tonight."

She had to agree. 'Business' did not seem a suitable topic of conversation in a place like this. They were seated outdoors at a table of the hotel's poolside restaurant. Strains of music filtered out from the nearby ballroom. The sky was generously dotted with stars. The moon looked very pretty in its first quarter. The night breeze whipped Koreen's hair and caressed her skin. Through a half-stupor caused by roast beef, red wine and chocolate mousse, she had to admit the place felt very romantic.

Over the past several hours, she thought about what he had said at the faculty room that afternoon.

If I had to choose someone to trust my dreams and lifeblood with, it would be the smartest, hardest working and scariest person I know. You.

She felt surprised and amused, but, mostly, incredibly flattered. His offer was something she was definitely considering. Being a Mathematics and Judo teacher was not her endgame.

There was something else, gnawing at the periphery of her thoughts.

He had chosen her. He trusted her with his dreams and his lifeblood.

Royce Duran didn't seem the kind of man who carelessly threw words around.

Did he think *more* of her?

She tested that theory earlier, after he had kissed her for the first time in all the years they had known each other. She kissed him, too.

Her only indisputable conclusion was that she wanted more of it all. She wanted more of him.

She did not want what he had, not really. She had never wanted to have his charisma or his leadership skills or his athleticism.

The realization hit her like a tidal wave.

She wanted him.

The coffee cup, mercifully empty, slid from her grasp, landing on the green turf under her feet. The dancing varicolored lights surrounding the hotel pool gave her a sense of vertigo.

"Koreen?" He was beside her in an instant, on bended knee, concern written all over his face. "Are you alright?"

She felt heat suffuse her cheeks. Her throat suddenly felt very dry. She swallowed and nodded. "I'm fine. I think I need to get out of here."

"Of course." He stood up and reached for his card inside the billfold. He had paid for the entire meal and given a tip. The numbers on the tiny piece of paper inside the billfold were so offensive, she did not even dare glance a second time. "You must be tired. Let me take you home."

Her hand shot out, landing on his forearm. "I don't want

to go home. Not yet. I never knew you were such a good loser. I want to find out more."

That was the best way of putting it.

Royce reached for her hands and helped her to her feet. His eyes were glued to her face, in what looked like a combination of fascination and surprise. She stared right back. She did not stop him when he pulled her close.

She did not stop herself, either, when she reached out and put her hands on his chest. Underneath her palms, she could feel his heartbeat, his breathing, and his body heat.

"What do you want to find out?" he asked softly.

The invisible line between them held, barely. If only she had the strength to break it.

"If you can lose in dancing, too."

It was two in the morning when they left the dance club of the hotel.

Royce parked the car in front of the gate as Koreen had directed. Behind the wrought-iron front entrance and concrete fence was a well-maintained two-story house, cream-colored under the streetlights, with large glass windows. He switched off the engine and turned on the car's overhead lights.

"My mother must think you kidnapped me or something," she said, rummaging through her handbag. "Can't imagine all her questions tomorrow morning. The perks of living with one's parents." She wrinkled her nose and feigned a shudder.

He remembered Koreen's parents very well. Her father was an architect, her mother a university professor. They had always treated him kindly, ever since he and Koreen were children. Her little brother, Kenneth, now a doctor in Family Medicine and completing residency in another province, was an old basketball buddy and, presently, a source of information on his sister's whereabouts (predictable) and relationships (non-existent).

His parents, on the other hand, adored Koreen. His father seemed to root more for her than for him, especially in Judo. His mother would always remind him to "go easy on the girl" or "keep an eye out for her."

Royce watched Koreen pull out her keys from the depths of her handbag. "The first time I had breakfast back home last week, I never realized how much food my mother used to make me eat. When I asked for coffee, she nearly threw me out of the house. She always thought coffee would stunt my growth."

"She's right, though. Looks like you listened when you were growing up." She laughed. "I would be happy to give her free one-on-one lessons on throwing, on the condition that she only applies her techniques on you."

"I wouldn't be surprised if she accepts, now that I'm around to actually throw."

"All my money's on her. She'll outrank you in no time."

They sat in companionable silence, her keys dangling in

her hand. He didn't make a move to relieve her of them, as a gentleman was supposed to do.

He didn't want the night to end. He still carried a vivid mental picture of Koreen dancing in his arms. She had been like a firefly the entire evening, generating energy all over the place. For probably the first time in their lives, they had done something together where they did not compete or keep score. They had just danced, plain and simple.

"Are you here to stay, Royce?"

Coming from her lips, his first name sounded foreign to his own ears. It was the first time she had called him that way. As far as he could remember, she had addressed him by his family name.

"You can say that, for the next few years at least," he replied. "I have to get permits and then start construction. After that, it's going to be a lot of work outfitting the Tower. I'll need to start recruiting a core launch group in the next month or so. I would have to travel back to Saudi later this year, to keep my visa valid. There are other sites to visit as well."

"Sounds very busy," she commented. "As promised, I'll think about your offer. It's too good to pass up, to be honest."

There was a change in her tone of voice. He searched her face. Still flushed from her night out, her skin almost glowed. "Please do. I'll be waiting for your answer."

He watched her shoulders rise and fall as she took a few deep breaths. "Well, thank you for the wonderful evening. I had a great time. I have never had this much fun since…I don't know. Maybe I've never had this much fun before." She shrugged and made a move to reach for her purple backpack.

It was his turn to stop her. "Koreen."

She paused mid-gesture, her cat-like eyes meeting his. "Yes?"

"Do you think we could be friends now? Start over?"

She picked up her backpack and slung it over her shoulder. "I'd like that," she answered, opening the door on her side of the car. She was on the pavement before he could ask anything else. "Good night, Duran." The passenger door shut in his face.

Why he had to be so obsessed with this woman, in the way he was right now, he had no idea.

"Wait." Fumbling a bit with his own door, he half-stumbled out of the car and made his way to her, catching up as she reached a small side gate.

"Koreen," he repeated.

"What?" Frustration was clear in her voice. The keys in her hand jangled loudly as she tried to unlock the gate. It didn't open.

It took him a second to see the reason for her failure. Her hands were shaking.

It took him one stride to get to her. He didn't take the keys from her hand, as a gentleman should.

He took her in his arms, brought his lips down to hers, and kissed her.

He was ready to lose. Lose his teeth, his bones, and, if she wanted, his heart.

Always unwilling to be outdone, she kissed him back. Just as a cat would, her arms and legs went around him tightly, possessively, marking her territory. He gladly took her weight, absorbing every bit of the heaven that was her and her touch.

When they finally pulled apart, panting, he was the first to speak. He didn't let her go. If she wanted him to, he would. But not yet.

"I'm sorry," he whispered into her hair.

Koreen was leaning against him, her head on his shoulder, her feet barely touching the ground. Her arms were still around his torso. She was breathing heavily.

"Are you?" She looked up at him, eyes blazing. "You're sorry for this?"

"No, I'll never be sorry for any of this." Unable to stop himself, he reached for her hair. The strands felt like silk on his fingers. Touching her was something he could get used to. "I'm sorry if this isn't what you want."

"I've wanted this for the longest time." She followed suit, reaching for his face, tugging at his hair.

Encouraged by her answer, he put his arms around her waist, pulling her even closer. "I didn't know what you wanted, Koreen. All you had to do was tell me."

"I think I did more than just tell you." Her fingers framed his face, holding him in place. "And you? What do you want, Royce?"

"I've wanted to impress a girl ever since we were children. I had to make sure she noticed me, but I was nothing compared to her. She is the smartest, strongest and scariest person I know."

"She doesn't think you're nothing," Koreen replied, smiling. "She thinks you're everything she has ever wanted, too."

He smiled back, his heart now in her hands. "If she wants me, I'm all hers."

"Good." She put her arms around his neck. It felt like a submission headlock and an embrace at the same time. "Now impress her."

"Now we're talking." He went in for another kiss, and maybe another one after that.

⁓

Koreen allowed herself to drown in him.

There was nothing to resist, measure or control. There was only the feeling of his arms around her, his lips on hers, his voice in her ear.

There was only a sense of triumph that, yes, he belonged to her, and she to him.

In the darkest hours of dawn, she felt the invisible line between them melt away, as if it was never there.

FOUR

Arrival

Someone was with her.

At the sound of footsteps coming up the porch, Tara's hands froze on the strings of the guitar she was cradling. Sitting cross-legged on the railing, she was enjoying her valued solitude in her family's ancestral home

She had deliberately decided to spend the year in the country to write songs and enjoy her own company. This was the kind of peace and quiet she rarely ever had in the city.

So much for peace and quiet, she thought.

"You stopped playing. I'm very sorry. Did I disturb you?" The voice was deep, male and sincere.

She glanced over her shoulder. The man looked vaguely familiar. He wasn't from the farm or the village, she was sure, but there was something about the way he stood and the way his eyes were shaped, almond-like and piercing, that made her feel like she knew him from somewhere.

"I wasn't expecting any more visitors," she said.

Earlier that day, there were a few people from out of town who had toured the farm. They had either been potential investors or existing exporters of the family's fruit preserve business. After a few weeks of being on her own, having company was exhausting.

She got off her perch and carefully placed her guitar in its case. She stood up, allowing herself to get a better look at the visitor. "Are you one of the exporters or—"

All coherence left as soon as recognition set in. It was like someone had slammed on the proverbial brakes, effectively stopping speech and breath. The years fell away, more than a decade of not seeing him in person.

Lucas Delgado.

Back in college, he was the star of the varsity basketball team. Two years behind Lucas, Tara had never been close to him, except that she regularly contributed her poems to the student publication where he was the resident artist.

The longer she looked at him, the easier it got to figure out how he had changed since then. He was bulkier and more muscular with age; taller, too, somehow, in the way he carried himself with quiet confidence. He used to slouch when he walked, usually clad in his seemingly endless selection of blue polo shirts.

A burning sensation formed in the middle of her chest,

at the sheer clarity of the memory she had of him walking in the university campus, carrying his ubiquitous grey backpack full of sketchbooks. Her heart skipped a beat when he smiled, seemingly unaware of the effect he was having on her.

"Actually, no. We're neighbors. Your foreman is a friend of mine. He let me in so I could pay my respects to you."

She stared. "You're friends with Fred?"

Fred was the third generation in his family to serve as foreman of the coconut farm. He and his wife, Marife, who was the estate's no-nonsense housekeeper, were among Tara's favorite people in the world, mostly because of how well they fed her. It was a highly valued custom in their town to provide abundantly to one's guests. To the couple, Tara would always be a guest of supreme importance, never mind that they worked for her family.

"Yes, I've lived in the village for the past couple of years. At least, my parents do, but I got them the house down the road. My father had always wanted to live here. He grew up in the next village."

He shook his head apologetically. "I'm sorry, miss. I think I lost all my manners on the way here." He held out a large yet graceful hand as he took a step closer, wavy hair tumbling over his high forehead. "Lucas Delgado. At your service."

"Tara Galvez," she replied automatically. She took his proffered hand, praying hers wasn't as shaky or sweaty as she felt it was.

"I know you from college," he said. "I used to draw for

the school paper. I think I may have done a few illustrations for your poems."

All she could manage was a weak smile, as flustered as she felt that very moment. Seeing Lucas Delgado after all these years, in her family's farm of all places, was a surprise. The fact that he knew and remembered her from college was a shock.

"Yes, you did. I remember. I think my mom had my first poem framed somewhere in our house. It had a drawing of a tiny boat on some kind of lake."

"Not my best work, to be sure." He grinned and finally released her hand. "I'm really sorry for barging in like this. I just came into the village this morning and heard from my mother that a famous singer was in hiding next door. I figured it was you. Galvez is a big name in this town."

"Not in hiding," she replied, amused. "My family owns this place. What surprises me is how you got Fred to let you in."

He looked somewhat sheepish when he answered. "Bribery. I would put good money on his choice in the next *fiesta*'s cock derby and split the winnings. I may have lost that money already."

"There goes years of my family thinking he's unwaveringly loyal."

"I'd happily take all the blame," Lucas said in an imploring tone. "I may have been a bit more pushy than usual. Please don't fire anyone. I'm a fan, so it's on me."

Today had brought one surprise after another.

He, of all people, had bribed his way into the farm to see her.

And he, Lucas Delgado, was a fan.

Tara shook her head instead. "It's fine. Besides, it's nice to see someone from college again." *Especially you,* she added silently.

"I'm surprised you remember me," he said.

Years of performing had taught her how to manipulate her facial expressions with supreme skill. She kept her face carefully controlled with a friendly half-smile. "I submitted my first poem to you, in freshman year. I kind of owe you my break in publishing, if you could call it that."

"Never thought I'd hear something like this from Tara Galvez, ever." The way he said her name was enough to make all the blood in her body rush to her face. "So, is my intrusion forgiven?"

She had to get her burning-hot face out of his sight, so she bent over to close and pick up her guitar case. She turned towards the horizon, past the seemingly endless rows of coconut trees, and saw that the sun was beginning to set.

"You will be forgiven if you stay for dinner." The words came out before she could stop herself. "Never let it be said a visitor left our farm without a proper meal. I would be disowned by my family otherwise."

"My pleasure. I'd love to stay for dinner."

"Do you mind if we go inside before it gets too dark?" She gestured to the wide sliding doors that led into the foyer.

"The staff should be getting dinner ready. It's just been pretty much me since I got here. I think they'd appreciate company."

"Let me get that for you." He reached for the handle of the case in her hand, deftly relieving her of it. For the briefest of moments, his fingers brushed hers.

She found herself gazing into his eyes, the closest she had ever been to him physically. Her throat felt tight. "Thanks."

He smiled. "Lead the way."

It was all she could do to keep her knees from giving out.

In the past hour, Lucas Delgado had reappeared in her life and basically overshadowed everything else in it.

As soon as they made their way into the living room, she gestured for him to sit on one of the couches and promptly excused herself, mumbling something about checking on dinner.

What was he doing here, of all places? What business did he have buying a house in the same town where she was supposed to find some semblance of tranquility?

What right did he have to make her feel as if no time had passed at all?

Tara took deep breaths as she made her way to the kitchen at the back of the house.

The house was a sprawling, hundred-year-old Spanish-style villa that stood at the edge of their family's coconut farm. Although Tara's parents kept the farm running, they barely stayed there and preferred living in the suburban area closer to the city, where they both ran a modest business in packing and exporting fruit preserves.

Tara herself had not even lived in the same province as her family for the past eight years. The youngest of three children and the only daughter, she was lucky enough to have been unconditionally supported in her chosen career as a musician. She had studied Business Management, in preparation for her role in the family business, and initially wanted to compose on the side and stay behind the scenes.

However, a demo tape where she sang her own song, 'Arrival,' unplugged, changed her best-laid plans in a heartbeat.

A year later, she was opening for an alternative band in the biggest Manila concert venues. Two years on, she had her own album and a three-night solo concert that was sold out in hours, quickly followed by another year abroad touring North America, Europe and Middle East. She barely had time to see her parents and friends when she returned to the Philippines. Instead, there was clamor for a new album, collaborations, guest appearances, and music videos.

Rather than spending her ninth year in the industry doing another concert tour, she had put her foot down and flat out refused, choosing to take a year's hiatus instead to write her third album before the demands of show business burnt her out at thirty years young. She chose to stay in her family's farm for this, much to the delight of her parents.

She had never factored in the presence of a man, much less this very man, in her self-imposed artistic exile. For all she knew, this was an elaborate matchmaking scheme of Fred's and his wife.

Not that Lucas was a bad choice, to be fair. He was a very successful professional athlete, not to mention famous and notoriously single. He was one of the highest-paid players in the country's major basketball league. He was traded to his present team about four years ago, where he'd since found his place in the starting lineup as one of the league's deadliest shooting guards. Last year, he was named the Finals Most Valuable Player of the All-Filipino Cup after leading his team to victory after seven closely-fought games.

She was going into her senior year of college when everyone started talking about Lucas Delgado joining the amateur draft of the professional basketball league. In the months that followed, he got picked in the first round by one of the country's most popular teams.

It came as a surprise to no one. Even though he attended the School of Business, everyone knew his heart and true skills were in basketball. Just like her, he found a career elsewhere, far removed from what he had gone to college for.

Tara would never admit to a soul how much she really knew about the man, how in the years since college she had quietly devoured every bit of information she could find about him. There was precious little about his personal life; Luke 'The Nuke' Delgado was an annoyingly private individual, according to the gossip columns. He was once linked to an actress whom he'd escorted to a showbiz ball, but nothing ever came out of it.

Just as nothing would come out of this, she thought, pushing open the heavy wooden kitchen door.

It didn't surprise her that Marife was standing there with the biggest, most supercilious smile on her sun-browned face.

"Good evening, Miss Tara. Would you and Sir Lucas like to eat in the dining room?"

Lucas watched her disappear down the hallway, never taking his eyes off her as long as she was within his line of sight.

Tara was very pretty, almost ethereal-looking, on her album covers and press photographs. Her beauty was even more striking in person. She had a delicate heart-shaped face, a slender build, and skin on the paler side. Her hair was the color of deep mocha, reaching down to the middle of her back. When she walked, it looked like she glided.

It occurred to him he was looking at her the same way he would look at the ball while it was in play.

Like any great idiot in the history of the world, he had let her go.

Tara Galvez was the reserved, obscure freshman who first stepped into the newspaper office hesitantly, all those years ago. He was putting the finishing touches to an editorial cartoon when she asked him where she could leave her poem for the literary editor.

He gave her a cursory glance and replied, "Just leave it on the table. Anything else?"

She shook her head. "No. Nothing else. Thank you." Then she fled, gone as quickly as she had arrived.

Curiosity triggered by such a painfully shy girl with the most melodious voice he had ever heard, Lucas momentarily forgot his deadline and turned to the piece of paper she had left. Once he read the opening stanza, he hurried to the corridor and tried to catch another glimpse of the girl.

To his disappointment, he could not see her anymore. With only her name written on the paper to go by, it took him a few days to track her on campus, what with its population of nearly two thousand students.

He saw her sitting on a bench outside the cafeteria, eating a sandwich in one hand and furiously writing on a notebook with the other. The stack of textbooks next to her had been enough to confirm his suspicions that she was a freshman.

At the time, they had been worlds apart from each other. He had everything a nineteen-year-old boy could ask for: immense popularity, the respect and admiration of teachers and peers, and a chance at the big sports leagues. He had a new girlfriend every three months, sometimes someone from another college department within their university, occasionally a girl from another school entirely.

If there ever was one thing that kept them connected, it was Tara's poetry, which she diligently contributed every time there was an open call for submissions. Up until his final year at college, no matter how busy he was, he never allowed anyone else to illustrate her poems.

He was in his fifth year in the professional league when he next came across her name. It was on a large poster splashed across the window of an entertainment superstore, showing an album cover with her face in profile: *Tara Galvez, 'Fragments of Us.'*

He bought that CD, as well as everything else she worked on in the years that followed. Lucas was pathetically grateful he had left his collection in Manila, safely hidden in the bedroom of his apartment. As with most single players in the league, he lived close to the basketball stadiums where the season games were usually held.

He was infinitely more grateful when he found out the very same woman was actually in the village where he was spending a month's vacation.

He had opted to spend his precious time between tournaments with his parents, rather than travel abroad and party way too much before their pre-tournament training camp. None of these would do his ankles and lower back any good, especially if he wanted to defend their championship in the All-Filipino Cup later that year.

The last conference had been the hardest run for him to date. Old injuries kept rearing their ugly heads. The other teams intentionally pitted bigger, taller, younger players directly against him. It seemed that all the other coaches had the unified goal of killing him slowly on the court, by breaking him down into useless pieces until there was nothing left.

Right now, the advent of foreign players and half-Filipino

kids in the league, all out for his blood, was the last thing on his mind.

Because, right now, *she* was there. He had never felt more at ease as he sat on the couch in her farmhouse, waiting for her patiently as if he had done so countless times before.

And, right now, there was no letting go.

A short while later, Tara returned and handed him a glass of chilled, fresh coconut water, which he accepted gratefully.

"When did your parents move here?" she asked, after informing him that dinner would be served soon.

"About two years ago, after my mother retired from government service. Around the same time, my dad decided to hand over management of the supermarkets to my brother. After that, they had the time of their lives organizing cooperatives around this area. They like it much better here, rather than the cutthroat life in the city."

Tara sat from across him, her eyes luminous in the shadows of the sunset filtering in through the windows. "I can understand. I have never slept or breathed better anywhere else, to be honest. It's a welcome change."

He nodded. "The very reason I come here, too, a few times a year if I can manage it. It's nice to rest and recover in a place like this. At my age, I would much rather be here than Boracay or Bali. Sounds terribly boring, doesn't it?"

There as a soft, knowing smile on her lips. "Perhaps in

the best way. Why do you think I decided to take a year off the entertainment industry and spend it here?"

"Great minds think alike, I suppose."

"Old, boring minds," she corrected.

He chuckled. "Imagine how the press would react if they found out we're both here at the same time, on vacation, in the depths of rural Philippines."

She cringed. "My manager would probably have me write a song about it. And shoot a music video with you on the farm. I shudder at the thought."

"Hey, take it easy." He held up his hands. "Am I that repulsive to you?"

She laughed. "I never said that."

A small parade of women walked into the living room, led by Marife, to announce dinner. They switched on the lights and insect repellent lamps, shut the windows and doors, and finished setting up the dining room. It didn't escape him how many glances and giggles the women threw his way.

Not that he minded. The best part was seeing Tara blush whenever she heard the giggles. She was very good at hiding her reaction, but every now and then he could actually catch a glimpse of how flustered she was.

Note to self: Get Fred a new motorcycle for Christmas. Or maybe get his wife something she wants for herself and the kids. Or get them all whatever the hell they want.

The fact that they had so willingly allowed him to intrude on Tara was worth their weight in gold.

That evening became the first of many.

In the weeks that followed, he became a fixture in Tara's life. He spent his early mornings jogging in the farm, after he had gained VIP access by bringing her the freshest bread from the village bakery for breakfast every day. In the cooler hours before twilight, she worked on her music at the front porch while he lounged from across her, idly sketching on sheet music she discarded. The evenings almost always ended with him staying for dinner.

On days Tara wanted to get out, Lucas would borrow Fred's motorcycle and take her wherever she needed to go. On Saturdays, his mother would demand for Tara to join them for dinner.

It wasn't too long before his parents started asking him loaded questions about her.

Would he see her again once the training camp started?

Did Tara have a boyfriend back in Manila?

Would Lucas visit them more often now that Tara was spending the whole year at the farm?

The questions, essentially the same and often asked repeatedly, hit harder and harder the closer his month was up.

The only question Lucas asked himself was: *How could he ever let go of her again?*

Today was her last day with him.

It was her first thought as soon as she opened her eyes.

As had become her habit, Tara woke up at sunrise.

She donned her robe and slid open her bedroom window, which overlooked a vast expanse of coconut trees and a small but colorful vegetable garden. Light was pushing out of the horizon in multicolored slivers. The air felt cool and soothing on her face. She only wished it could soothe the emptiness she felt inside, too.

It was Friday. Early tomorrow, Lucas would be traveling to the provincial airport to catch his flight to Manila. He would arrive in Metro Manila very early Sunday morning, just in time to get ready for his team's training camp starting that Monday.

She knew his schedule by heart. She had, after all, arranged for one of the farm's service vehicles to take him to the airport. She had taken it upon herself to do this because his parents, who had gotten used to having him around, were not taking his departure too well. Yesterday, she caught his mother crying over a framed picture of five-year-old Lucas. His father had spent the past few days poring over the books of the local cooperative, refusing to come out of his library for meals.

They were not the only ones who had become attached to Lucas' constant presence.

She knew, however, that although sentimentality made her lyrical work such a beautifully heart-rending success, it got her nowhere in real life. Her songs were her emotional haven, a cocoon of safety from disappointment and heartbreak.

She had tried, once, in the US. He was a Filipino-American from Los Angeles, whom she met at the kick-off party of her North America concert tour. He had followed her to other states for weeks, laid his heart at her feet. She gave him three weeks and broke up with him in Washington D.C., shortly before she flew to Toronto. It didn't feel right to string him along.

But what about him, now?

She had to ask herself that question, although she had no honest answer.

She had pined for this man nearly half her life, watched and adored him from afar, robbed herself of the chance to experience something else with someone other than this tall, wavy-haired creature of her dreams, whose piercing eyes had never stopped haunting her.

Over the past month, gone was the memory of a lanky, slouchy Lucas walking around campus. Instead, what lived in her head were more vivid snippets of their time together. Lucas bringing her *pan de sal* under duress; Lucas sneakily sketching her when he thought she wasn't looking; Lucas laughing at the dinner table at some silly anecdote she had shared, promptly choking on a mouthful of chicken. This time, the images were punctuated by the sound of his baritone voice; the scent of him in that cologne he endorsed, sometimes mixed with sweat; the warmth of his body as she held on whenever he drove her around on the motorcycle.

This was as real as it could get.

She felt a tear slide down her cheek.

Damn him. Why was it so hard for her to let go of him, more so now that she knew him so much better than she thought she ever could? Their newfound friendship, if one could call it that, made everything worse this time around.

To her horror, she saw the real Lucas running up the garden path, clutching a familiar brown paper bag. She quickly dragged her hand across her face and pulled her robe tighter around her body.

"Someone's hungry," he half-shouted from the field, waving when he caught sight of her. "I hope you got the real coffee this time, not that three-in-one swill."

She waved back. "You bet. I'll see you downstairs."

They had *pan de sal* and freshly brewed coffee on the front porch. They spoke of everything and nothing, from village news on which politician was rumored to be the patron of the next *fiesta*, to the weather conditions that might potentially delay his flight to Manila. It had been humid that side of the province these past few days; it was only a matter of time before it rained.

It was midmorning when Lucas finally got to his feet, after they went through the entire bag of bread and two pots of coffee. She was tempted to reach out and pull him back down, just to make this time last longer.

"Are you coming back this afternoon?" The words, to her own ears, sounded like a plea, a losing bid. She had never heard herself sound so pathetic. "I'll have something special made for you, that *biko* with the sweet coconut shreds and *calamansi* you like you much. Whatever's left you can bring with you tomorrow."

He shook his head. "I'm so sorry, Tara. My parents

wanted to take me to the next village for lunch with their old friends and cousins. My dad insisted. At least he's talking to me now."

"It's okay, you should go," she said, in sharp contrast to the way she felt the pit of her stomach cave in. "I'll get the *biko* made anyway. You can eat that to carbo-load before your training camp starts. I'll make sure it's packed and ready to go tomorrow."

"Sounds good," he replied with a grin. "Why don't I bring over dinner tonight? Marife and the other ladies could use a break. Let me treat you instead. It's the least I could do."

Relief mingled with melancholy and despair at his words. She had only been awake for a few hours yet she felt drained at the emotional toll his impending departure took out of her.

"Sounds good," she echoed, willing herself to smile. "Enjoy your lunch, then. I'll see you this evening."

"I'll be here at seven." Before she knew what he was doing, Lucas bent down and kissed her on the cheek. She felt his hair, damp and soft, brush against her temple. His lips were warm on her skin. "See you tonight, Tara."

She watched him walk away, back down the path through the vegetable garden, disappearing into the rows upon rows of coconut trees. Once he was out of sight she finally did what she could never do in front of him.

She let the tears go.

now and forever

Lucas was at the farm gates shortly before seven that evening. It was very quiet, except for the sound of crickets chirping. Gone were the night breezes he had gotten accustomed to. Instead, the air was heavy with humidity. It felt like he was already back in the city.

Fred was waiting for him. "Good evening, boss."

"Good evening, Fred."

"Looks like rain's coming this way. Would you like for me to leave the motorcycle by the garage? I can pick it up from your parents' house tomorrow."

Even Fred's normally cheerful demeanor was gone, replaced by a more somber, resigned expression. His face seemed to look more weather-beaten under the bright lights coming from the large lampposts.

Lucas nodded. "Sure, that would be great."

"Miss Tara asked me to go with you to the airport tomorrow morning. We already have your *biko* ready. The driver and I will pick you up at nine. Is that okay?"

He had to ask. It seemed as if time was moving more quickly and he was losing grip, all over again. "Fred, is everything alright?"

"Yes, sir."

"Don't 'yes, sir' me," Lucas snapped. "I'm not your sir, I'm your friend."

Fred was looking at something very interesting on the ground. "Yes, sir."

He sighed and put a hand on the older man's shoulder. "What's wrong, Fred?"

"It's none of my business, or anyone's, really."

"Then what is it?" It took all of his patience just to get the words out.

"Miss Tara." Now, Fred was looking down at the well-worn baseball cap he clutched in his hands. "Do you care for her? We thought you did. I mean, we would never have let you meet her if we thought you didn't have honest intentions. My wife and I are responsible for her. I have worked for her parents since she was a little girl."

Lucas felt his entire body tighten. He never knew emotions could cause such physical pain.

"My intentions have always been honest," he said through gritted teeth. "Where is this coming from, Fred? We've been friends for the past two years. You know very well I'm not that kind of man."

"Miss Tara is a very special girl." Fred met his eyes dead on. "It would take a blind man not to see it. If you don't intend to come back for her, very soon, then you are not the man I thought you were."

He had expected a threat or some kind of warning. Something about him not breaking Tara's heart, or the whole village would descend on him like a rabid mob.

Not this.

There was a long pause between them, punctuated only by the heavy silence of the humid night.

"I love her," Lucas finally admitted. "I think I've loved her for a very long time."

"Good," Fred shot back quickly, sounding strangely like his coach. "So tell her."

~

So tell her.

The words hung over his head, long after he had said goodbye to the foreman and made his way to the house.

The house was very quiet. It was a little darker than usual, enveloped in the night except for the bright lights left open on the front porch and in the living room.

He rang the doorbell.

She opened it after a few seconds. Her eyes looked bigger and brighter than usual, her cheeks paler in stark contrast.

"Hi," she said softly "Good evening. You made it."

"Good evening." He stepped inside and held up the bag full of grilled food he had procured from the next village. "I hope you like barbecue. I have enough in here for a whole team and then some."

Tara closed the door behind him. Instead of taking the bag, she promptly went in for a hug. It was the first time she had put her arms around him, at least when they were not speeding down a highway on the motorcycle.

She lingered, not saying anything. Not that he was complaining about it.

Instead, he put his free arm around her shoulders and pressed his lips to her hair. She always had the scent of vanilla, which he liked a lot. "I'm sorry I couldn't spend this afternoon with you."

He felt her shaking her head against his chest. "It's alright," she mumbled. "You're here now."

Lucas carefully reached over and put down the bag of food on a nearby side table, making sure he did not break contact. Now that both his arms were free, he enfolded her in them, hoping she would not resist.

When she didn't push him away, he pressed small kisses to her forehead and temples.

In response, she held on to him tighter.

"Hey," he said into her hair. "Are you okay?"

She did not answer. Instead, she turned her head upward, to look into his eyes.

What he saw in her gaze was answer enough for him. He brought his lips down to hers. She was soft and damp, even better than he had imagined her to feel.

Tara kissed him back, more passionately than he had ever dared hope for. He felt her reach up, sliding her hands up his arms and shoulders, trying to wind her own arms around his neck. He bent down to her height, bringing her closer to his own body, until she was wrapped around him as if she was the only one who had ever really belonged in his arms

So tell her.

He eased his tongue into her mouth, tasting her. Her tongue met his, sweet and hot and willing. She had the intoxicating flavor of fruits and the mountain breeze. Nothing had ever tasted so good.

He knew that kissing her would not be enough. Not this time. Not ever again, if he had his way.

He wanted all of her.

He moved his hands from her waist and into her hair. The locks were soft and thick, something between silk and velvet, as he ran his fingers through the strands.

With each moment, her body grew warmer in his embrace. The sweet vanilla scent of her was all over him, from her hair, from her skin into his own.

His lips left hers, allowing them to draw breath. In the shadows, her eyes were glittering, the pupils dilated, dark lashes fluttering as she panted against him.

She groaned in protest, making him smile. She had excellent cardio. Even if he was a career athlete, she was giving him a run for his money.

Her hand on his nape, she pushed him back in to continue the kiss, this time their lips and tongues meeting and clashing more forcefully. Her other hand moved to his chest, small noises coming from her throat as her fingers reached under his shirt and wandered over his bare skin. She didn't stop until she reached his stomach; she continued until her hands were on the waistband of his jeans. To his surprise, she reached boldly inside.

He was already hard as a rock, but he stiffened even more under her touch. If she kept this up, he would come soon, right there in her hands. His breath came in short hisses as he looked into her eyes, to see her reaction.

Her eyes were wide as she rubbed the whole length of him, deliberately slow in her movements.

"Oh," she said against his lips. "You're so-"

He didn't let her finish. He had to do something to level the field. One hand firmly on the small of her back, he reached for the hem of her dress and pulled it over her head, revealing her bare chest.

He chuckled in satisfaction when he saw she wore nothing underneath her dress but a small patch of cloth for modesty, already clinging to her mound. The light was sparse, but it showed him enough.

She wanted him.

They fell in a frenzied tangle on the wooden floor, kissing and caressing each other, clinging to each other as their borrowed time came to a hazy, heady standstill.

He determinedly pulled off her underwear and cast it across the room. The sight of her laid bare before him, moaning and raising her hips, was nearly too much.

"Tara."

He didn't know if her name, spoken in a hushed, shaky voice, was an apology, a plea, or a prayer. Perhaps all three.

She reached up, her fingertips light and cool on the scorched skin of his cheeks and jaw.

"Yes."

He didn't know if her response was an acceptance of his apology or consent to his heart's most fervent desires.

He wished, desperately, that it was both.

"Don't stop, Lucas," she breathed. "Not now."

There was an inexplicable lump in his throat.

"Tara, I—"

She silenced him by wrapping her arms around his neck, crushing her mouth against his.

So he told her how he really felt, the best way he could. He showed her.

❦

He forgot about dinner, so did she.

He knew there was a lot unsaid between them, but their bodies spoke louder, much clearer than words could.

Lucas allowed himself to forget about the rest of the world, too.

It was only that night that mattered. In those moments, he never let go of her. Even when exhaustion took over them, he made sure she fell asleep in his arms, before he drifted off himself.

He woke up before sunrise. It took him a moment to get his bearings. He was in another bed, in another room.

Tara.

He reached for her, instinctively feeling for her warmth. The spot next to him was rumpled; her pillow still held that lingering scent of vanilla he now knew all too well.

His first coherent thought was his confession she had so smoothly suppressed.

Or perhaps denied.

Tara, I love you.

How desperately he had wanted to say it.

He'd promised himself he would tell her in the morning. But she was no longer there

There was a small stream of light coming in from the hallway. He realized they never really had the time to shut her bedroom door.

He went to his feet, feeling slightly shaky and very, very hungry.

It took him a while to find all his clothes. He never found her, even after scouring through the entire villa as best as he could.

He was exhausted and frustrated by the time it was first light. He finally made his way to the front of the house, gaze lingering on the bag of food that had gone cold, untouched, on the very same table he had set it down upon.

Propped up next to it, however, was something that wasn't there before.

It was a silver disc, in a transparent plastic case. It had no labels or pictures.

There was only one word on it, written in black marker: *Lucas.*

For the last three months, she found it got easier and easier to hide.

She had started that fateful night, when she spirited herself away into the old warehouse next to the garage. She heard Lucas leave on the motorcycle.

Since then, Tara barely left the farm, if she did at all. Her time was divided into two significant segments in a day. In the afternoons, she wrote songs on the porch, scribbling lyrics in her notebook or testing chords on her guitar. In the evenings, she recorded in the makeshift studio she had set up in one of the empty rooms on the ground floor. She had pretty much moved out of her bedroom upstairs and into the studio, where she usually slept in the morning hours.

Almost halfway into her year's sojourn, she had written fifteen songs, enough for an album concept.

Music was her haven, after all.

It wasn't too long after that she sent out her demo tapes to her manager, who had promptly gotten a producer to look into possible arrangements. Her record label was over the moon at the richness of the new material.

For whatever it was worth, she had paid the price, many times over.

"Miss Tara?"

At the sound of Marife's voice, she looked up from her computer, away from the overly enthusiastic email of her manager.

"What's up, Fe? I'm too tired to meet anyone, please. It's been a long day."

"Madam Mercy called again," said the housekeeper, in a cautiously even voice. "I said to her that you were busy with your demos, as you told me to."

Mercy Delgado. Lucas' mother.

"Thanks, Fe," she said gratefully.

"She said she does not believe me anymore, Miss Tara," the housekeeper continued.

Tara was silent. What could she say? Did she have anything to say?

"She left a message, too. She asked if you would be so kind as to watch the Finals game tonight and the press conference after. The team of Sir Lucas will be playing."

Tara looked away, back at the computer screen, not really seeing anything except words and phrases popping up here and there, out of her manager's message.

Emotional gravitas. Maturity. Different woman. Surefire hit.

"What time is the game?" Tara finally said.

"It will start at eight. I can set up the TV in the living room for you, if you like."

Television sounded like an alien contraption to her. In the entire time she was at the farm, she had never even touched it.

"Please, Fe. Thanks." She looked at the housekeeper and gave her a slight nod in dismissal.

Another call.

Tara thought they would all have given up on her by now, including Lucas and his mother. He called almost every day. The last call from him was this morning, around half-six. She had been asleep. His mother called at least once a week, most of the time on Saturdays.

At eight, she forced herself out of the studio and into the living room. The TV was already tuned in. It didn't take her long to realize it was the seventh and last game of the All-Filipino Cup finals.

"Luke 'The Nuke' Delgado, what a well-fought tournament he has had," a commentator was saying. *"If they win tonight, he will, without a doubt, be taking home the Finals MVP trophy again. He has dealt with all these injuries, right and left, and stayed in the starting line-up without even flinching."*

The screen zoomed in on Lucas. He was wearing the familiar white jersey, with the number one on it. He was shooting lay-ups at the tail end of the team warm-ups.

The other commentator chimed in. *"Before that, let's talk about all these rumors going around that they will be announcing something big about The Nuke at the end of this game. Will he be traded again? Or will he be retiring, at the peak of this career? What do you think, Doug?"*

A sports analyst was beamed in from a television studio. *"Your guess is as good as mine, Benny. Let's not forget there are other teams outside of the country that would benefit from his skills and experience. He is a legendary player and would make a formidable coach."*

Tara turned down the volume as a cold chill ran the length of her spine.

In one way or another, Lucas was moving on, just as she had expected he would. Someone like him would never really stay put, when there was something greater that awaited.

She watched the muted screen for the next two hours. Midway through the game, there was a charging foul from a member of the opposing team that could have very well broken Lucas' ribs.

By the time the last two minutes rolled about, Tara's breath had nearly left her body. Through the haze of combined excitement and dread, she turned up the volume when the scores tied.

Lucas' team had possession of the ball thirty seconds before the final buzzer. A teammate tossed him the ball from the inbound line. The seconds ticked by as the shot clock started running down. Twelve to shoot. Eight. Someone stepped in front of him; he evaded easily. Six. Two players tried to block his way. Four seconds. His hands came up, lightning-quick. The ball hit the board, then spun around the hoop.

Pandemonium erupted when the ball swished through the net.

"Luke Delgado. Three points!"

The other team had six seconds to shoot. The ball moved quickly, almost desperately. It never had a chance, with Lucas in its way. The bigger offensive guard made the shot but Lucas stopped the ball in mid-air, in what looked like a resounding block.

"'The Nuke' blocks the shot," said the TV commentator. "And it's over! Game clock is down to zero. We have a champion!"

And it's over, Tara thought.

She settled back into the couch, remembering this was the exact same spot he had sat on when he first came into the house all those months ago. Memories. That was all she was ever meant to have of him.

It felt bittersweet to watch him celebrate with his team and receive the Finals MVP trophy. It took a full hour, and countless interviews later, for the press conference to start. There was another half hour of accolades and praises, with the team owner enthusiastically sharing his plans for the rest of the season.

It was nearly midnight when Lucas, dressed in a pristine white suit, entered the venue with the team manager. All attention turned to the new arrivals.

Lucas and the manager sat next to the team owner at the table. As soon as they had settled, questions exploded from all over the room.

The team manager held up a hand, a diplomatic smile on his wizened face. *"Luke Delgado will be making a statement to our ladies and gentlemen of the press. I would be happy to address all your questions after."*

Lucas stood up and walked to the podium. Her heart caught at the sight of him. He was undeniably, heartbreakingly handsome, at nineteen or thirty-three. She could only imagine how much adoration he commanded at the moment, how many people would fall at his feet. It was enough to make her feel, strangely, jealous.

"Good evening," he began, with that charming grin she had grown so familiar with. *"Or is it good morning?"*

Appreciative laughter rang throughout the room.

He acknowledged the audience, and continued by thanking his team for all their efforts not only through the tournament but the entire season. He singled out a few people by name. He went on to praise the other team, as any good sportsman would.

"I'm sure everyone has heard one or two rumors about how I would end the All-Filipino Conference, aside from partying with my team." Another round of laughter. "Please allow me to put these rumors to rest."

"I will not be joining the Arabian Falcons in Abu Dhabi as their coach, or in any other capacity. I had a generous offer from Sheikh Khalfan, which I had to regretfully turn down. My heart is in the Philippines and in this league."

Tara could hear murmurs rising from the crowd, even through the screen.

"There is no trade in my future, not in the next tournament or the following season. I won't be a free agent either. My contract is with my team, and that is where it will end."

The buzz from the audience was getting louder. She realized that she, too, had inched to the edge of her seat, attention completely riveted to the screen.

"I am ending the All-Filipino Conference with my retirement from basketball. Tonight was my last game. Being a part of this championship legacy has been the greatest honor of my career. From the bottom of my heart, I would like to thank the millions of fans all over the world for your love and support. None of this would have been possible without you."

Voices were raised all over the room, mostly in shock and unabashed curiosity.

Lucas went on. "I will still be the league's biggest fan, but I would no longer be playing or working in it. It's time for me to become a spectator to this sport I have loved since I was a little boy. Once again, thank you." He lowered his head in a bow, hand over his heart.

He was about to step away from the podium when one particularly loud reporter shouted out a question over the din. "What's next for you, Luke?"

Lucas looked straight at the reporter and smiled. *"Maybe music videos. Who knows?"*

It was a week after the Finals game.

The past days had been uneventful. No calls, except from her parents and brothers. They were making plans for Christmas, still a few months away. Yes, she would be here if they wanted to celebrate at the farm.

Tara sat cross-legged on the porch, idly strumming her fingers through the strings of her guitar. She was supposed to be arranging a pop ballad version of her first song, 'Arrival,' the final track of her third album. The label wanted a more contemporary spin to the song, which they called 'Arrival, too.'

Today, however, the remake held very little of her interest or attention.

Instead, she thought about the sixteenth song she had written, the only one she had not shared with her manager, or anyone else for that matter.

The demo for the sixteenth song was a gift, given to the only person who was meant to hear it, saved in a CD and hurriedly left, in a torrent of tears, for him to find. She had not played that song for months, not since she made the demo the afternoon of his last day with her.

She took the guitar pick from her shirt pocket and started strumming the opening chords. She could remember them well enough. Ever since Lucas left, she had not looked at the lyrics or sheet music of this particular song. She didn't have the heart or courage to.

But now, memory and melody flowed effortlessly.

She began to sing.

You said that you were sorry
That you don't need me no more
You said that you were leaving
And walked right out the door

Baby, how many times have you hurt me?
I truly have stopped counting
How many times have you left me?
Standing alone while it was raining

You said that all was wrong
That nothing works when we're together
You said we would only be lying
If we keep talking of forever

So go on, tell me
Whatever you want to say

Go on, be true
There seems to be no other way

Tell me I'm not the ideal
I know all your reasons why
Tell me I'll never be strong
That I'm always lacking in your eyes

Tell me everything that hurts
This forever hopeful heart of mine
Tell me how to make you stay
But, baby, just don't tell me goodbye

She had barely completed the last note when she heard footsteps coming up the porch.

Someone was with her.

Tara's hands froze on the strings. She did not dare look over her shoulder. It could be anyone, couldn't it?

His voice told her otherwise. "You stopped playing. I'm very sorry. Did I disturb you?"

It was different this time. It would be different.

She jumped to her feet and put the guitar away, as fast as she could.

"Lucas."

She said his name, almost disbelievingly, before throwing herself into his arms, in affirmation that this was no longer just a memory.

"Hello, sweetheart," he said, in that gentle baritone that

had whispered so many beautiful things to her. "I missed you. Where have you been?"

"Hiding," she answered, honestly. "Hiding here. Hiding behind my music." This time, the tears came, no longer in her power to control.

"I tried to reach out. I tried to call. Why didn't you answer?" His tone was very tender, more so his embrace. These were enough to break her.

"I know. I'm sorry. I didn't know what to do." The sobs came, wracking through her body. "It's always been just me and my songs. Nothing was real."

He held her until she was considerably calmer. "Your song," he finally said. "Everything you wrote. All those feelings. They were all real, weren't they, Tara?"

"Yes."

"Since when?" he prompted.

"Since the beginning," she answered shakily, but without hesitation.

He put his hands on her shoulders. "Was it the time you handed over that first poem, all those years ago? For me, it was. You never once left my mind after that."

Tara remembered that day, how quickly she had run for her life after seeing him at the newspaper office. She shook her head. "It was the second week of freshman year. You had on a blue shirt and you were running to the basketball court. Your backpack, it was grey and full of sketchbooks. One of them fell out. I picked it up and tried to give it back. You didn't hear me so I followed you. I was so scared to go near the court. Everyone was there; the athletes, the popular girls."

"I waited for your practice to finish. It had barely started when it began to rain. Everyone ran for shelter. So did I, but I didn't get very far when I slipped on the ground. You saw me then, and you saw your sketchbook."

"You didn't laugh or say a word. Instead, you picked me up and carried me to a nearby classroom. You took your sketchbook back and gave me your varsity jacket in exchange. Number one. Then you ran off. Your jacket kept me dry and warm and I…never forgot about it. I never forgot about you."

Lucas shook his head. "I still have that jacket."

"I got it washed and brought it back. I gave it to one of your teammates. I told him I found your jacket in the quad."

"You should have given it back to me," he said, reaching for her face and her hair.

She leaned into his touch. "I know I should have. That would have saved us a lot of time."

"Maybe. But time is what I have plenty of, Tara. Every minute of which I wish to spend with you. Starting now."

Realization dawned, slowly, a warmth that spread from her heart to every single fiber of what made her whole. "You retired from basketball—"

"To ask you to marry me," he finished, sliding his hands around her waist to draw her close. He began to kiss her, starting with her hair.

"I don't want you to give anything up for me."

"Give up?" He paused in his kisses long enough to stare

at her. "I stopped, Tara, because basketball was killing me. I'm not that young collegiate gun anymore. I barely made it out of the tournament alive. Maybe you are killing me, too, but it feels way better."

"You love basketball," she protested, weakly.

"Not as much as I love you," he countered, his lips nuzzling at her temple.

"What's next for you? Music videos?"

"If that's what you want. If you don't find me repulsive." There was laughter in his voice. "Otherwise, I have invested in our family business and the local cooperatives my dad is helping. I have even invested my income this season in Galvez Farms. I think I'll be fine."

She pressed closer to him as his lips found their way to her cheeks and nose. "Yes, you will be fine. More than fine."

He finally captured her lips with his own. He dove in for a deep kiss before he took a step back and went down on one knee. "Please, can I propose now?"

Her heart in her throat, she nodded. "Yes."

"Is that your answer, then?" In his hand he held the most beautiful ring she had ever seen. The diamond, surrounded by what looked like sapphires, formed the sail of a tiny golden boat. The band was golden, too, softly curved to mimic water.

"Yes," Tara said, as he slid the ring onto her finger. "I love you, Lucas Delgado."

She went into his arms, into his kisses, into all of him—the past, the present and the future.

She knew, then, that she was never letting him go.

FIVE

Aflame

"Lissa? Something wrong?"

She shivered slightly as a gust of wind disturbed the comforting stillness of the summer evening. She closed her eyes, luxuriating in the darkness just after sunset, and felt the soothing cricket sounds wash around her. Spending time in her mother's garden, ensconced in her favorite rocking chair, had always been comforting.

"Lissa?" Russell Suarez placed a gentle hand on her arm.

Pushing an unruly strand of hair away from her face, she finally turned her attention to him. She knew he had been standing in the garden for at least five minutes, quiet and observant. She wondered if he knew what she was thinking about.

"Hi. I thought you were packing for tomorrow's flight."

She managed a little smile as she stretched and got to her feet.

"It leaves early. And you still have to sit through my special *Bon Voyage* breakfast. Don't forget that."

Russell, like Lissa, was a writer. That was where the similarities ended.

He was the star columnist of a big national daily, where he wrote *Man on Fire*, an opinion segment that took on current issues and events on an entirely different, if not controversial, spin. The vacation he had taken this week was one of the very rare breaks he took from his job.

If he wasn't writing his column, he was covering national and international events. The last one had been the regional economic summit, serialized in the newspaper and syndicated in other media outlets.

On the other hand, Lissa was a freelance writer and proofreader, on top of her job as an English tutor for foreign students. She stayed in her hometown and did work here and there. She occasionally got breaks from bigger publications and had several contributions in magazines.

"Your breakfast offer is something no person in his right mind would refuse." Russell's soft brown eyes twinkled. He was as handsome as a 1940s movie star, with longish black hair framing a chiseled face with what she called a 'Hispanic' profile.

"Flatterer." She quickly averted her gaze.

"What's wrong?" he insisted. The man really was more sensitive than she gave him credit for. "Is something wrong?"

"I haven't eaten much today," she admitted, allowing him a small portion of the truth. "I don't feel like having a bite, though."

He placed an arm around her shoulders. "You sure do look pale. Why don't you come to my house? I actually came over to see if you wanted to join us. My cousins are having this big feast of *lechon* and *talaba* in my honor."

"Do you mind if I stay here for a while?"

"No, not at all."

She became quiet, leaning her aching head on his shoulder.

"So, Lissa." He cleared his throat.

Curiosity made her lift her head to look at him. He couldn't meet her eyes.

"I hope you don't mind me saying," he continued, a little more quickly than his usual relaxed manner of speech, "but you've got to take care of yourself more. Your mother told me you're fond of staying up until dawn and drinking gallons of coffee."

"I work better at night. You know that." She wrapped her arms around herself and stepped away from him.

He sighed and tried to reach for her hand. She pulled it out of his reach. "We're all concerned. I suggest you take it slowly. Don't be too hard on yourself."

"I like my work." She was beginning to feel defensive.

"Easy," he said, sensing her distress, holding up his hands. "I don't want you to get mad at me for caring about you."

Caring about you.

The words registered, but she refused herself the hope in them.

Russell was her oldest friend, someone who called during special occasions and sent her chocolates, flowers, and silly cartoon cards on her birthday. His unexpected intrusion into her routine, if not downright dull, life mere days ago had certainly been unsettling. He had spent most of his time with her, endearing himself even more to her.

"Please, Lissa," he went on pleadingly. "Don't be mad."

She sighed, defeated. There was no point in picking a fight with an unwilling opponent. "I'm sorry. Migraines make me cranky."

"Don't apologize. Come here."

He put his arm around her shoulders again, this time bringing her closer. He placed a kiss on the side of her head. As far as she could remember, he had always touched and held her like a protective older brother.

They had been close since childhood. They grew up on the same street and attended the same schools until they both finished university with degrees in Mass Communications. Their mothers were as close as sisters, too; they worked in the same government office and had both been widowed at a fairly young age.

How could she even get mad at him in the first place?

In spite of how much he had outdistanced her career-wise, Russell had never once made mention of it. Earlier that week, he had read over her tentative writing ideas for one-off feature pieces and praised them sincerely. A few days later, she had found herself talking on the phone with a pleasant-sounding woman, the lifestyle editor of the same newspaper Russell wrote for.

"Please send me your pitches for articles, Miss Garcia. I was very impressed by the samples of your work Russell sent me."

As easily and as quickly as he had breezed back into her life, he had changed it, too.

She didn't know if it was for the better, though. Not if he, just as quickly and just as easily, would leave it again.

She was as cold as ice.

The Lissa he knew very well was not this detached shell of a woman who barely said a word and disappeared into herself. She was the person he had most looked forward to spending time with during his vacation, one he had fought so hard and given up two big stories for.

The past days with her had been wonderful, enough to recharge him for the next few months of relentless work and travel, ungodly hours of writing, and even one or two anonymous death threats.

Regardless of what he was going back to, Russell didn't want to leave Lissa in the state she was in. Or he damn well wouldn't leave at all.

"Why don't we go somewhere, just like old times?" He suggested, pleasantly, trying to break through that strange wall she had put up. "I don't think I can eat any more *lechon*, to be honest, not if I want to run the marathon again."

Russell felt her discomfort as she disengaged herself from him. Had he done or said something wrong? He wracked his brains, going through the events of the past week, and came up with nothing.

Lissa hesitated. "Okay. We just have to make it back before midnight, though. My mom will tell your mom, and then they will both panic. You know how they are."

"The park, then?"

"Okay. Give me a minute and I'll meet you outside." She turned and went inside the house.

Russell, shaking his head slightly, made the short trip next door to his own house. His cousins had brought over a videoke machine; they were now singing a slightly off-key version of *'Skyline Pigeon.'* A few slices of pork and empty shells remained on the dining table.

He took the keys of his mother's car and left word that he was driving out for a while. His mother had, apparently, gone out with Lissa's mother to some ladies' club meeting.

"Russell has a hot night with his girlfriend," a cousin gleefully declared on the microphone. He ran out of his own house, followed by catcalls and whistles. He made a mental note to ask his mother to ban everyone inside from ever coming back.

His face still felt hot when he spied Lissa standing outside their gate. She had changed into a new blouse and jeans, and was carrying her handbag. He quickly went into the car and backed out of the driveway before his cousins could see and tease her, too. That would probably make her mad again, and she would most likely take it out on him.

To his relief, they made it out of the neighborhood without drawing attention. They were on the coastal road within minutes.

He gave Lissa a quick sidelong glance. She was seated a little too stiffly, her eyes on the darkened highway outside her window.

"Remember where we used to take this car when we still worked for the college paper?"

She nodded, her eyes still turned away from. "To the all-night *arroz caldo* place. Too bad they had to close it down. I miss it sometimes. None one else in town makes chicken soup like that anymore."

"We'd pool our coins together sometimes and split the serving," he added.

Lissa finally looked at him with a small smile. "And split the egg. Don't forget the egg."

"Yellow for you, white for me." Up until now, he would only ever eat the white portion of an egg. It was a habit he had picked up from all those years of sharing *arroz caldo* with her.

Silence wrapped around them. Russell turned on the radio, letting soft music fill the dark car interior. A short while later, they pulled into the parking lot of the seaside park. It was one of those places where children could play on the waterfront and shutterbugs and artists alike could catch a clear, unhampered view of the sunset or sunrise.

Ever since he could drive, he and Lissa would come to the park during the unlikeliest hours of the day and write their assignments, bingeing on half-gallons of Rocky Road bought by whichever one of them had allowance left.

The park was not very busy in the late hour. There were a few groups, mostly families and couples, scattered throughout the lawn overlooking the sea. He stepped out of the car and opened the door on her side. He wanted to hold out a hand to help her, but decided against it. She had been averse to physical contact earlier. The last thing he wanted to do was push her further away into herself.

He slowly headed for the huge stone platform built next to sea, hoping she would follow. He was relieved to see her fall into step beside him.

"I wish the rest of the gang were here," Russell said, pointing out a row of swings and naming their closest classmates from university. "Bobby, Claire, Freya and Dale. They would have attacked those kiddie-sized swings already."

The remark made her considerably relax. He could see her shoulders lose some of their stiffness.

"They have kids who attack swings now," Lissa said. "I saw Bobby and his wife in Church last month. They have three kids now. What a difference a few years could make."

"Maybe more than a few," he offered.

"Has it really been that long?" Her voice was soft, distant, almost wistful. "It feels as if time moves without me sometimes. I keep on missing out on the good stuff. It's like everyone else is living their lives out there, and I'm stuck in here."

Her words stopped him in his tracks, as if he was shot in the gut.

What could he say?

More importantly, what could he do?

Lissa had stopped walking, too. They stood in silence, looking out to the sea, until he felt her hand in his.

"I'm sorry for ruining your last night at home," she declared softly. "I shouldn't have said anything. I imagine I sound as depressing as hell."

"No, you don't." Her hand felt cool, damp and delicate. "You sound very real."

"My problems are not your problems."

He turned to look at her. She was bathed in moonlight, a heartbreakingly beautiful wisp of a woman with the darkest hair, gentlest face, sharpest eyes and most honest soul he had ever known.

His Lissa.

There was only ever one answer. "I could make them mine."

Lissa's heart thundered in her ears.

She had been wading through dangerous waters earlier; she was now treading the deep end.

Russell Suarez was not supposed to be there, with her. He was supposed to be on another high-flying assignment, a familiar name on a national byline, a larger-than-life presence on a page that took no prisoners.

He was not supposed to be *this* real, not anymore.

She thought he had gone on to live his life without her in it, just like everyone else had.

"You don't know what you're saying, Russ." Lissa let his hand go and wrapped her arms around herself. This was now her default defensive reaction, to whatever it is the man in front of her made her feel.

It was a mistake agreeing to come here in the first place.

Just as he was in his writing, Russell was unforgiving. He rounded on her. "The least you could do is give me a little credit, Lissa. I do know what I'm talking about sometimes."

"You think you know anything about me?" she shot back in frustration. "That, somehow, after a week, you could make everything better?"

"Is that what you think I want to do? Change your life? Do you think I want to be some kind of self-sacrificing hero?" He stood so still but was filled with so much passion he was practically on fire with it. This was the side of him that could turn a whole tide of sentiment, the side of him that made people take notice and listen. "I couldn't change anyone's life, least of all yours."

"What do you want to do, then?" Tears began to spring in her eyes, brought on by his fiery reaction, her fears, and the ties that bound them to each other.

"I want to be a part of your life, Lissa. I want to be there when you feel you're stuck, or if you don't want to move."

"Why?" She choked out.

"You know why." His voice was so soft she could barely

hear it over the sound of the waves crashing against the shore. He need not say anything more. His gaze held all the answers.

Her hands fell limply to her sides. It felt harder to keep her feet rooted to the ground. Breathing was difficult, because, in place of the cold emptiness inside her, she was filled with so much feeling, all at once.

Wonder. Disbelief. Heat.

Love.

As with all fires, it took only a single spark.

She didn't know who moved first. She only knew she was back in his arms, but this time, his lips were on hers, his hands were in her hair, and she was melting into him, the same way he was into her.

"I hope you know what you're getting yourself into," she breathed against him.

His face was fierce, as his hands were gentle on her body. "I know I'm exactly where I'm meant to be."

There it was, in his eyes, as clear and blinding as the sun burning in the midday sky. If only she had tried to look before, maybe she would have already found it.

It didn't matter now.

She had found him, and he had found her.

SIX

Angel

STRANGER

She gazed at the sky for probably the umpteenth time in the past hour.

It was a starry night. The North Star and the many known constellations stood out clearly, brightly. The moon was bright and perfectly spherical. There was no chance of rain.

It was the kind of night for romance, at least for a teen-aged girl.

Estella Montero sat by herself at the street corner. The bench, with a newly dried coat of fresh paint, courtesy of a congressman, was right by the bus stop.

This was her favorite intersection, one she had grown up

in. It was always brightly-lit by traffic lights and neon storefront signs. Green, red, orange, yellow and blue; it was its own kind of rainbow.

A gust of wind blew, stirring the street before her. Discarded newspapers and fliers flew by, tumbling on the stone pavement decorated by graffiti as colorful as the lights overhead.

Stella looked at the sky again. In mere seconds, it seemed to have grown murky and cloudy, as if someone had stolen the lights.

The stars were not the only ones that disappeared that night. Her hopes had gone, too.

Was it only this afternoon when Aaron called and asked if she wanted to go to the movies with him? Was it only a few hours ago when she, drifting on fluffy white clouds, had put on her best dress and favorite shoes and snuck into her mother's room to use her makeup and perfume?

She had already fallen from those clouds. More like stumbled, fell, and landed on the cold hard ground on her ass.

Six-thirty, the time she was supposed to meet Aaron Soler, had come and gone.

It was getting cold. She looked at her watch. It was already half past eight. She pulled her now-rumpled white cardigan more tightly around her body, shoving her hands into their shallow pockets. She would be an idiot if she allowed herself any more hope that he would show up at all. She had more self-respect than that.

"Stood you up, hasn't he?" The voice came out of nowhere, causing her to nearly jump out of her skin.

She sprang to her feet and backed a few feet away, hands clenching into fists as she turned to face the owner of the voice.

She had a box cutter in her bag, she thought, comforted. A girl who grew up in a city like hers knew how to protect herself.

He emerged from underneath the awning of an ice cream shop.

It was a boy. No, a man, tall and dangerous-looking as any predator of the shadows.

He had a thick mane of hair that fell past his shoulders. His skin was duskier than most, allowing him to blend easier into the night. Most of his face was still shrouded in the darkness; what she could see was about a third of his profile, sharp and harsh.

He was the most fearsome and compelling sight she had ever laid eyes on.

"Who are you?" It was almost a shriek, nothing like her own voice. "What do you want?"

He advanced into the light. His face looked even harder and older. There was a scar that ran the length of his right cheek, hidden in part by his long hair. He appeared to be in his early twenties, perhaps older.

"My name is Trey," he said, almost formally. "Hello, Stella."

She backed further away, hot and cold rushing through her veins at the same time.

"How did you know my name?" she demanded.

He gave a slight shrug, his shoulders rippling. "I asked."

She drew herself to her full height of five-foot-five, enough to intimidate most boys her age. It would probably have no effect on him, seeing that he was much bigger, but there was no harm in trying to appear braver than she actually was. "Asked who?"

"The people here. Everyone knows you."

"The people?" she echoed, stumped.

"You see them every day."

She stared, trying to understand what he meant.

Them? The people?

She blinked, slightly taken aback by the bright light coming out of the open doorway of the leather repair shop down the street. She shut her eyes for the briefest of moments. When she opened them, she saw the sweet old woman who ran the shop give her a smile and a friendly wave. Seconds later, someone else left the shop, the old man who did all the repairs by hand or using an ancient pedal machine.

She watched them lock up the shop and walk off.

She understood.

This was her intersection, her neighborhood, her city.

"Yes," she said, more to herself than to the stranger. "I see them every day."

"So you do."

She glared up at him, feeling infinitely more confident

that she did minutes ago. "That doesn't explain why you're here, or what you want from me."

"With you? Nothing." Trey sat on the bench she had vacated, draping his arm over the back of the seat and extending his legs. With his dark shirt and jeans, he looked like a giant snake, coiled and poised to strike. "Why I'm here has everything to do with your friend, the pretty boy."

"Aaron?"

"We were tipped off by one of his sidekicks. They come here and pick up girls for their pot sessions. The last one didn't go so well. Joshua didn't want to be part of the repeat performance."

'Pretty boy' Aaron, who was supposed to be her date, was a senior and the most popular boy at their college. His father was the mayor of one of the smaller towns that bordered the city. Aaron always had a lot of boys in his entourage, mostly those from more affluent families; they moved around the school as if they owned it. Girls who got his attention instantly became the most popular ones at school. With her being only a freshman, his initial attentions had flattered Stella to no end.

"Joshua." She repeated the name, trying to jog her memory. "He's the one with the red car. He was supposed to pick me up tonight, with Aaron, and…" Her voice trailed off.

"Joshua Benitez won't be coming, either," he said. "As for Aaron Soler, let's just say his plans have changed."

Girls. Pot sessions. Repeat performance. His words kept echoing in her head as she stood stock-still on the sidewalk.

This time, she shivered for real. The night breeze was nothing compared to the cold coming from within her

"Did you want to sit down?" Trey moved his arm out of the way and slid to one side of the bench.

Stella hurried over and plopped down next to him, before she collapsed from the sheer weight of information she was absorbing.

"How long has this…been going on?" So many questions popped into her head, but it was difficult to put them into words. This was the kind of urban cautionary tale picked up and sensationalized by late-night crime investigation shows. "How did you know about them? How the hell do I know you're even telling the truth?"

"I don't have to answer any of that, do I?" He leaned forward, placing his elbows on his thighs and clasping his massive hands between them. He turned his head and peered at her face. "Or would you really want me to?"

She found herself looking into his eyes. They were midnight-black, unblinking. Strangely, she felt no discomfort under his gaze; instead, she stared right back.

"I just wanted to go on a date with Aaron, you know," she said softly. "When he asked me out, I was on top of the world, everyone at school was looking at me. They all saw me. And Aaron…he actually knew who I was, he got my name right and everything."

"I'm sure he did." There was no sympathy or sarcasm in his voice. He sounded as if he didn't have to convince anyone of anything. "He knew Victoria, Yasmeen, Jennifer and Grace very well, too. Unlike you, they never stood a chance."

Stella didn't know the other three, but Jennifer Ang was a sophomore Aaron had dated the previous semester. She was a beauty queen, slated to compete in the national circuit of pageants that coming summer. Shortly after Jennifer and Aaron broke up, Jennifer's parents, who both worked abroad, had pulled her out of college in the middle of the year and brought her with them to Singapore. There had been rumors of a pregnancy, a party blunder that displeased her sponsors and ruined her image, an expulsion notice that was kept quiet…

"I knew Jennifer," she said. "She's a beauty queen who used to go to my college. She was his girlfriend for a while. She left town end of last semester."

"She got lucky. Grace was from about six weeks ago; she was studying Political Science in the university across town. She sat where you are sitting now. They saw her here before she got in the car with Benitez. She's in rehab now."

The strange reality of it all was overwhelming. In a matter of hours, she had been stood up in what was supposed to be the biggest date of life, her great crush had become a junkie who was bad news for girls, and a stranger from out of nowhere had appeared to be some twisted version of a guardian angel.

"Do you know where Aaron is?"

There was a crooked smile at the corner of Trey's mouth.

"Do I really have to answer that question? The less you know, the better for you."

"I can't just sit here without knowing anything," she insisted. "If you want me to at least believe in what you're trying to tell me, then give me some answers."

"Soler won't be able to come here tonight. He and his friend are both at the docks. I brought them there earlier. We're trying to get them to sing. If they're lucky, they would get a little beaten down. If not…" He shrugged. "It's not like they even cared about what would happen to those girls."

"And you…you got them there?"

"It's my job. I work for the man who decided to put them there and, at the same time, get you out of something you wouldn't want."

She sat next to him, trying to keep her breathing even. She had somehow stumbled straight into the plot of a cheap action movie. At any other time, this would have felt contrived, even cheesy.

But she felt nothing like that.

This was a close call, not a joke. She could have ended up like any of those girls.

At that moment, Stella wanted nothing more than to see her mother. If anything happened to her, she could not even imagine her mother's reaction, the pain it would cause her. Even thinking about it made her feel *guilty*.

"I think I want to go home," she said.

The intersection was almost empty except for a few pedestrians and the familiar nighttime vendors who sold peanuts, duck eggs and green mangoes from their baskets. Most of the stores were already closed for the night. She had been there for almost three hours.

"I'll walk you there." He stood up the same time she did. Side by side, she barely made it to his shoulder. "Or wait until you get into a taxi."

"That won't be necessary," she said, flustered. "I live a few blocks away, near the commercial port."

"You can walk on your own if you want. I'll follow, anyway, and make sure you get there."

At any other time, she would have found those words creepy. She would have felt uncomfortable at the very least.

Tonight, however, was the kind of night that brought creepy to shame. If anything, she was past creepy.

With Trey, there was no feeling of discomfort, only a sense of awareness that he was more intimidating than everyone and everything else around her.

"Fine," she said, thinking she would rather have someone like him walking her home, rather than the less impressive assurance provided by her box cutter. "Let's go."

CRIMINAL

She looked at the sky again, maybe for the seventh time in the past half hour.

It was still raining. It showed no signs of letting up.

Stella stood by the waiting shed next to the main gate

of her college. She was still mercifully dry, if not for errant drops of rainwater, brought about by nasty gusts of wind, whipping against her skin and her white college uniform.

This wasn't rain, she thought. This was a full-blown storm, at least Signal Number Two.

Night had been upon them for hours, with clouds blotting out the sun since mid-afternoon. All the classes for the evening finished at seven-thirty. It was already past eight.

The campus would be locked up soon. She would have to brave the storm on foot and wade her way through the flooded streets if she didn't want to get kicked out or get stuck. It was only a matter of time before the water levels got too high, if the rain didn't stop.

It was a simple, straightforward plan. Out the school and through the city's main street, where there was better drainage. She could use the buildings as shelter and sprint the last few hundred meters home past the plaza and the church. She would be soaked to the bone and maybe even get sick, but at least she wouldn't freeze to death outside her own school.

She turned to the other students huddled next to her, looking them over as she took off her shoes. There were three other girls and two boys, all looking as if they had the same predicament as she: brave the rain and flood, or wait it out. Her own choice already decided, she put her shoes in her bag and gave them a silent nod before walking out into the downpour.

It was easy enough to cross the road and make her way

past the market. She was able to take shelter in the windows and awnings, up to and until she reached the main street.

By the time she made it to the intersection, the rain was so heavy she could barely see past a few steps in front of her. The shops had closed, with most of their lights and signs put out. What little light there was came from the streetlamps that still worked. She could feel water, cold and sticky, running in quick tiny currents under her feet. Blasted on all sides by strong winds, she could barely stay upright. It was like being in the middle of a sunken, vengeful city.

So much for her plan of using the buildings as shelter. She'd be lucky if she could make it past this junction. One wrong step could lead her into an open drainage hatch, if she didn't fall on her face, drown or get electrocuted first.

She stood in front of the sixty-year-old grocery store, squinting through the rain at a dim light coming from the window of a single shop across the street.

It was the old couple's leather repair shop. Were they still there? Could she possibly stay with them until this was over? Could she even cover that much ground without dying along the way?

Throwing caution literally to the winds, she drew her bag tighter against her body and sprinted full speed across the darkened road. Her bare feet burned from the roughness of the asphalt and the icy coldness of the flood.

"Hello? Can I please come in?" she called out, half-crashing, half-stumbling against the shop entrance. She pushed the wooden door open with all her strength and promptly ran into a wall.

She felt the wall give way a little, then something grabbed her upper arms, steadying her. It took her a second to figure out that she had run into someone, not something.

"Stella?"

It took a few more seconds for her eyes to adjust to the soft yellowish light inside the shop. Through a haze of stinging rainwater, she could make out a large black figure with equally dark hair and eyes. His face was the last thing that came into focus.

It was him.

"Trey?"

"What the hell are you doing here? Are you okay?"

She flinched at the harshness of his voice, or maybe at the strength of the grip he had on her. She could barely move her upper body.

At least she could still move her head. She nodded. "I'm fine. Can you please let go of me?"

His hands loosened and fell away. She watched him take a step back, inwardly debating with herself whether or not this was all real.

"Did I hurt you?" Without taking his eyes off her, he picked up something from the front counter. It was an emergency lantern, the source of light she had seen through the window. The shadows in the room shifted as he brought the lantern overhead.

"No, it's okay," she replied, a little too aware of how

closely they stood to each other. The repair shop had always been tiny, but now it felt considerably cramped and tight. "Where's Auntie Yolly and Uncle Frank?"

"They've gone home. Did you come here to see them? All the shops closed hours ago." There was a note of disbelief in his voice.

She shook her head. "I was going to take shelter here. It was the only place with the lights on. I thought I could get home on foot, but the streets are too badly flooded."

Exhaustion and cold started nipping at her joints. She leaned against the wooden counter and put her bag on top. Her uniform was drenched, the skirt stained by the flood waters.

It was only then that she noticed it.

The blood.

Next to the space where she had put her bag, she spied small streaks of dark red liquid. Her eyes followed the stains over the side, all the way down the floor, to the spot where Auntie Yolly would usually stand to serve customers. Concealed behind the wooden counter were two limp bodies leaning against each other, their faces split open like overripe watermelons.

She screamed.

She tried but never got the chance. He put his arm around her and brought her close to him, pressing her so tightly against his body that any sound she could make was muffled against his chest.

"Stella," he said, very calmly, almost soothingly. "Stella. Stella, look at me. Please don't scream. Just look at me."

She could feel her body shake violently at the gory sight she had just witnessed. She focused on his voice, the welcome heat of his body. She was fine. It was just blood. It wasn't her blood.

"Look at me, Stella," he repeated. "Don't scream. They're not dead. I won't hurt you."

Clutching at his shirt, she willed herself to open her eyes.

She could see, under the light of the lantern he held up, that he was looking at her, too, into her eyes. His own eyes smoldered like hot coals. She focused on them. He wouldn't hurt her.

"Good," he said. "Now breathe."

She breathed out, a long exhale that made her lightheaded. She held on to him, kept her eyes locked onto the somehow comforting familiarity of his face, as she tried to get her bearings.

"Please get me out of here," she heard herself say, trying very hard not to think of the bloody pulps next to her.

His face impassive, he let go of her and moved to the entrance to bolt it shut from the inside. When he was done, he gestured for her to go further inside the shop. "Let's go upstairs. If the water gets any higher, we'll be safer there."

Still feeling sick to her stomach, Stella carefully took her bag and did as instructed. Beyond the front of the shop, behind a thin plastic curtain, was the small workroom she was familiar with, lined wall to wall with tools and Uncle

Frank's ancient pedal machine. To one side was a narrow flight of steps.

Guided by the light of the lantern, she was able to find her way to the mezzanine in record time. It was no larger than the downstairs area but had a higher ceiling. It appeared to be some kind of storage room for the shop's supplies. At one end of the room was a large glass window.

She put her bag on a shelf and made her way to the window. There was almost nothing to see, except the rain pelting against the glass and a very limited view of the flooded street outside. Most of the working streetlamps she saw earlier had gone out.

"You should sit down." Trey had put down the lamp on a tiny table and was bringing over a wooden stool for her. "You didn't have to see what you just saw. I guess you'd want an explanation?"

She settled on the stool, stretching out her legs and bare feet. She looked at him as he backed up and settled his large frame on the table next to the lamp. He looked bigger than she remembered; his hair was longer, too.

It didn't surprise her that he was talking so casually about the scene downstairs.

"Did you do that to them?" she asked, boldly.

"I did, just before you got here," he answered. "As I said, they're not dead. They're just out. I remember doing the same thing to your old friends a while back."

She remembered that night vividly. After she'd reached home, she had looked over her shoulder to see Trey gone.

She had tried not to think about what had happened and had not told anyone, not even her mother. In the Monday that followed, there had been a large ruckus at the college about the two boys and the rest of their circle getting arrested. None of their gang of nine ever made it back to campus. As far as she'd heard, the other boys had been caught in the act of using drugs and hurting girls from other schools. Stella had thought that maybe Joshua had sung a little too well, or maybe Trey and his boss had made him do so.

"What did they do this time? Drugs?" Stella tried not to think of all the blood splattered on the counter and the floor.

"They were going to burn this building down. They got into the shop by breaking the front lock. They probably wanted to make it look like an accident that started from here, with the amount of leather oil they were carrying. They could have easily taken out this entire block, too. These buildings may look like solid stone from the outside, but inside it's all old wood."

"Why would they want to do that?" She thought of all the people who had stores in the block. She had known most of them since she was little; if not by name, she recognized them by face.

"Territory. Those fuckers are not from here, they're not even from Visayas. They're the Zamora family from Manila. They want to control the Pier District, starting with the small businesses. With the livelihood of the people gone, it would be easier to buy them out."

Trey got off the table and walked the length of the room

to look out the window himself. "They tried the same thing last month at the port, with the vendor stalls. We barely got there on time. Otherwise, they could have burned down nearly two hundred stalls and parts of the commercial port."

She lived there. Her house was a stone's throw away from those stalls. She used to eat there regularly. "The only thing I heard about the port was that there was a huge riot that broke out among drunks over videoke. It was all over the news last month. My mother warned me not to go there in the evenings once they start all the singing and drinking."

He looked over his shoulder at her. "It was a good story, wasn't it? The boys staged the riot so well and got all the attention. We were lucky at the time."

She hesitated before asking her next question. "What are you going to do about them?" She gestured vaguely downwards.

"We're tracking down their friends who could be in the other buildings. As soon as we could get through the flood, we're taking these sons of bitches to their quarters across town. It took us a while to find out where they're holed up. Turns out they live in the house of Greg Garces. He's got ties with the Filipino-American mafia. I wouldn't be surprised if he's the one funding this little takeover attempt."

Another cause, another enemy.
More blood.

Why Trey did what he was doing she had no idea. "What do they want from the Pier District? I've lived here all my life. Most of us in our neighborhood have. It's just boats and warehouses and shops, and tiny old houses like mine."

He turned to face her completely. "Whoever controls the district controls the shipping routes and traffic. What goes in, what goes out, what everybody does in it. Most importantly, who gets to do business. All kinds of business."

"Somebody already does that, right?" She searched her memory for the name. It was a very old name, the elusive but notorious family that owned at least half of the district where she lived. "The Esguerras?"

"Raphael Esguerra. Ever since he took over a few years ago, other families and groups have been trying to take him down on all sides. A new leader usually takes a lot of heat. We've been putting out fires for a while now."

"You do dangerous things" she said. "You could get killed. Can't you just…quit?"

"And do what?"

"I don't know. Live and work somewhere else."

"Some of us can't just quit," he said with more emotion than she'd ever heard. "Some of us can't just give up the life we were born into. I grew up in the docks. I've lived here my whole life, too, just like you. I will do everything in my power to keep the Pier District from getting destroyed by outsiders, even if it means becoming a criminal to get rid of the people in my way."

His eyes left her then, as he focused his attention back to the window.

She stood up and picked her way over to the window,

to see what he was looking at. It was still windy and raining heavily.

"I hope it stops raining soon. I want to go home. I've been at school since eight this morning."

"Aren't you cold? You look like you're going to be sick soon." The concern on his face made her aware of their closeness.

All she had to do was reach out, to touch him, to make sure he was real.

Ever since that night at the intersection, she had thought about him constantly, wondering if he ever existed at all. She had wanted to ask others about him, but had decided not to. She knew if he'd been just a figment of her imagination she would be devastated.

She was soaked with rainwater and freezing all the way to her insides. She wasn't even aware she had wrapped her own arms around her body to keep herself warm.

"I'm fine. It was my fault. I forgot my umbrella at the library. By the time I came back to get it, I was too late."

"Here." Trey started unbuttoning his shirt. She stared, heat rushing to her face. She tried to move her legs, to step away from him, but she was frozen to the spot. His black shirt opened, showing a grey t-shirt underneath. He took off the polo and handed it to her. "Put this on."

She was blushing and she knew it. The grey shirt had a tighter fit on his body. His shoulders and chest were broad, contrasting with his flat stomach and narrow hips. His black polo ended up in her shaky hand.

"Thanks," she heard herself choke out.

"I'm sorry if there are any…stains on it. I don't have anything warmer."

His shirt was the warmest thing she had ever touched. It had a clean, fresh scent, something like pine, tinged with the sea. She slid her arms into the shirt, almost disappearing into its considerably larger size.

"It's fine. It's very warm. Thank you."

They both stood by the window in silence, staring out into the rain and the nearly invisible city street.

"How are you, Stella?" It had gotten so quiet, his voice almost startled her. "I didn't get to ask you earlier."

"Life goes on, I suppose," she said. "School has been busier since I was a freshman. Thankfully, no one tried anything since that night. I think everyone got a little bit scared with what happened to Aaron and Joshua."

"A little bit scared?"

"Scared shitless, then?"

"Better."

She smiled. "So, how are you?"

He held up his left hand to the light. His knuckles looked freshly skinned, with a little blood caked and dried on them. "Bloody after my little fun. I guess I'm fine."

She was tempted to reach out and touch his hand. She could only clench her own fingers into a tight fist.

"I don't think I ever got to say thank you," she said.

"For what?"

"For back then." She could feel herself blushing again.

She really had to get herself under control. All this caused by someone she barely knew, someone who had the knack of appearing out of the darkness for her, whenever she needed it most. "And for now, I think."

He shook his head. "You're thanking me for showing you two half-dead bodies in a leather repair shop?"

"For being there, Trey. It means something to me, even if the thought had never crossed your mind. Don't be like that."

She was rewarded with the tiniest of smiles. "This is as much of a surprise to me as it is to you, Stella."

The moment was interrupted by his phone ringing. He took it out of his pocket and answered. "Yes. I'm still here. Are you sure there's no one else out there?"

Trey looked out the window again. "Can you drop someone off first, then come back? Good."

"There's a car on the way," he said to her, replacing the phone in his pocket. "It can get through the flood. They'll take you home."

"That's great. Thanks." She looked around her, never at him. He would disappear again for goodness knew how long. She had to say it. "Will I see you again?"

He was already making his way back to retrieve the lamp from the table. He stopped mid-step and stared at her from over his shoulder. "What?"

"Will I ever get to see you again?" she repeated, as bravely as she could.

"Why would you want to see me? People don't usually like seeing me."

"I like seeing you," she retorted.

"Give me your phone." He walked back to her and held out his hand.

She reached into her bag, between rows of damp notebooks, and retrieved her phone. It was only slightly damp on the outside. The tiny device almost disappeared into his hand.

He looked at her phone's casing for a few seconds. It was made of shiny white silicone, decorated with a stylized drawing of a black archangel. He didn't comment. He turned it over to the screen side and started typing.

She heard his phone ringing again. "That's you calling. I'll save your number. Call me whenever you need, okay? I will answer."

She was tempted to say something in response when he handed the phone back to her. Nothing came out of her mouth. Not even when she retrieved her bag and followed him down the stairs.

She stood as close as she possibly could to the entrance, the farthest from the two bodies behind the counter. Trey was talking on his phone again, to someone else, about meeting them in another district across town.

It barely took any time before the car reached the flooded main street. She saw its headlights approaching and turned to him.

Stella finally found her voice. "Thanks." She took off his shirt and handed it back.

He shook his head. "No, keep it."

"I don't think I can." *Even if she wanted to.* "My mother will ask a lot of questions. It's a very small house. And it's just the two of us."

"Don't worry. I understand." He took the shirt and put it back on just as she heard a muted honking from outside. He unlocked the shop's front door and held it open for her. "Take care of yourself."

"You, too." She walked past him and stepped back into the street. Once outside, she could see that the rain had calmed down. It was still pouring heavily, but she could barely feel the wind.

He followed her. "Tell Mario where you want to go. He'll drive you there."

A dark four-wheel drive had stopped outside the shop. It stood amidst the flood looking like a tank. A middle-aged man rolled down the window by the driver's side and was about to step out when Trey held up a hand and opened the backseat door himself.

"Good night, Stella." The rain dripped on his face and hair. He didn't even blink.

She finally reached out and got to touch his left hand, the one with the skinned knuckles. It felt warm, rough, strong. "Thanks again. Good night."

He nodded and shut the car door. He didn't move from the spot where he stood, not even when the giant car pulled out of the sidewalk and started making its way through the flood.

She never took her eyes off him. Not until the sight of him was swallowed by the darkness that stretched out behind her.

RECKONING

She looked up at the sky, then down at her watch. She sighed, trying to find a more comfortable position on the bench. Her legs and feet, clad in the black regulation stockings and low-heeled shoes of her school uniform, felt cramped. She felt warm in the white suit and regretted not changing into something cooler.

In the early evening, the intersection was the same as always, bright, messy and full of people rushing to catch a ride or selling food and trinkets. There was a thick, balmy breeze coming from the nearby waters of the docks, heavily tinged with salt. It was going to be a humid night.

Was it only a few years ago that she had sat on this same bench, shivering in a white cardigan, grappling with the dark realities of the world she was growing up in? It felt like a lifetime ago.

She wasn't surprised when someone suddenly took the spot next to her on the bench. She kind of expected it.

Stella had expected anything to happen since she got the text message from Trey last week. She had never called or messaged him in the past eighteen months since they last saw each other. She had not deleted his number, either.

It was the only message she had ever received from him.

> **Can we meet**
> **Same place**
> **Friday 6pm**

She had called him back straightaway, just to make sure it wasn't someone else messing with her. He had answered after two rings, in that deep, raspy voice that sometimes followed her, especially when she walked alone in the city streets at night. Sometimes she dreamt of that voice, too.

For this Friday, she skipped her last class and told her friends she would meet them at the movies tomorrow evening. She had the foolproof reason of completing a report due that Monday.

"Hi, Stella." Trey, no longer a disembodied presence at the back of her head, looked surprisingly different. His long hair was tied back in a neat ponytail; he was dressed in a green polo shirt, blue jeans and brown shoes. He looked almost normal; his scarred face was as fierce-looking as ever, maybe even a little sharper with age.

Stella wondered how he thought she looked. She had definitely gotten taller since last time. Over the past few years, it was her height that brought her attention and sometimes opportunities neither she nor her mother had ever expected. A few months ago, she was approached by an events company to model for a local fashion show early next year.

"How are you, Trey?" she asked, politely. Light conversation had never been part of their interactions.

His Adam's apple was bobbing up and down. "I'm fine. Thanks for coming. I didn't think you would even answer my text. How have you been?"

She forced a smile, as strange as it felt to have normal small talk with him. "Good. Busy. Reports and exams take up most of my time. I'll be graduating this school year."

There was a rustle as he pulled out something from behind his back. She was certain he had gotten even bigger since last time; his shoulders looked wider in the more flattering cut and color of his shirt.

To her surprise, there was a small box of roses in his hands. There were three: one red, one pink and one white.

"I didn't know which color you liked, but I took a chance and picked roses," he said. "You always have on some kind of cologne that smells like roses."

"Yes, I like roses," she answered, taken aback. "Roses are nice."

If she had to list a hundred things this man was capable of doing, giving her roses would never even be a remote consideration, much less knowing how she actually smelled.

She reached out to take the box, trying to think of something else to say and failing miserably. She wasn't sure if she had intended to touch him, but her hands landed on top of his.

She looked up into his dark eyes and, sure enough, they were on her, too. She understood that look from a man, far better now than she did four years ago. No matter how mysterious he appeared to be, he was still a man, wasn't he?

"I wanted to see you," he finally said, breaking the silent, unmoving exchange between them. "I didn't want to leave town without telling you."

Her fingers closed around the box. It was made of white cardboard, plain yet sturdy, with a plastic display window to showcase the flowers inside. It was something she expected from someone like him: unadorned and straightforward.

"Where are you going?"

"Does it matter?"

"It does to me." She clutched the box closer to her, pressing it to the space between her chest and her stomach.

"I'm going to get a few things out of the way. North, mostly in Manila. We've lost a lot of good people to the Zamoras this past year. They haven't stopped trying to take over the Pier District."

His back heaved in what looked like a sigh. "It's only a matter of time before this escalates to an all-out war. But Iloilo is our home, we were born and raised here. We won't give it up, so we're bringing the war to them."

He was bringing the war to them, she thought.

Stella suddenly felt cold, empty, abandoned. The same way she had felt the first time she met him, on this very bench.

"You'll be back, right? You said before this is the life you were born into. You can't just leave, can you?"

There was that familiar tiny smile at the corner of his mouth. "It's not about leaving or staying. When I chose to do this, I knew I wouldn't be coming back. Sometimes, there are things we need to do that we can't just walk away from."

"I see," she said, evenly. "You'll be missing my graduation, then." It sounded stupid and pointless, but nothing ever made sense with him anyway. She could not even fathom how deep, dark and bloody the world he lived in was.

"I guess I will."

"I was a freshman when we first met, you know."

He nodded. "So, are you going to the senior prom with someone special?"

"Prom?" she echoed. "I haven't really thought about it. I don't have a special someone."

The idea had never really crossed her mind, not since what happened during freshman year. She had nothing against boys in general, but since then she had been averse to the young adult rituals of courting and dating.

Sure, there were a few boys who showed interest, some more than others. Darryl, whose family moved from another province at the start of their junior year, had been courting her shortly after he completed his first semester at the college. He was part of the student council and tutored younger students in Math subjects. Her mother liked him immensely. Stella didn't exactly dislike him; she just wasn't interested.

"It took me a while to trust boys again, after what happened. But I've learned a thing or two since then. I would stick an idiot in the throat with a box cutter before they could try anything funny." She had to smile through the heaviness in her muscles, a strange sensation considering how empty she felt inside.

They sat in silence for a while, before he stood up.

"I'm glad you're okay, Stella. At least I got one thing right in all of this."

Driven by a sudden sense of panic, she jumped to her own feet. "Are you going now?" she blurted out.

"I'm leaving tomorrow morning, so I'd better get ready." He was looking down at her with his mouth in a thin line. "I'm sorry if I bothered or upset you in any way. If there was someone I had to say goodbye to, it was you."

She felt something rise in her throat, bitter and painful and stinging hot.

Goodbye, she thought. It sounded so final and absolute.

Guardian angels were supposed to stay, weren't they? Wasn't he supposed to stay with her?

"I'm glad you told me," she said honestly. "It gave me a chance to see you. I thought I'd see you again sooner, after last time. But I'm glad you're here now."

"Me, too."

She swallowed hard, trying her best to stem the flood rising dangerously fast from within her. "It's early. I skipped my last class to meet you."

Before he could respond, she continued. "Let's eat something, okay? It will be my treat. I never had the chance to do anything for you."

Without giving him the opportunity to refuse, she grabbed him by the arm and pulled him through the throng of people milling the busy nighttime streets. She knew this place was part of him. This was home for Trey.

They had dinner of grilled fish and rice at a small, open-air eatery on the docks. It was nice to see him doing something normal with her, for a change.

Or for the last time.

It was almost nine in the evening when the lights of the stores and restaurants started going out, signaling the end of the day. She thought back to the time she had sat at the intersection and looked at the dying stars as her own hopes died, too.

Trey was the only constant presence between then and now, between an innocent teenager's disappointment and her first real heartbreak.

Her twisted kind of guardian angel, who was leaving her life as soon as the day was over. She was determined not to lose any more time she had left with this beguiling man.

"You live near here, don't you?" She had her hand

on his arm, a gesture she had dared to try earlier, as they walked on the open pier, the area where smaller passenger boats docked in the daytime. She had thought he would not want to be touched, but she was wrong. She was glad to be wrong.

"It's near the old Customs office," he said, a little too formally, nodding towards a cluster of warehouses a block away. "My boss bought a few buildings here to keep some of the cars and for us to stay in if we wanted. I didn't want to live out of town."

"Can I see your place?" Heat flooded her face at her own boldness.

He stopped in his tracks. "It's late. I should be walking you home.

"I don't want to go home. Not yet."

"What do you want, then, Stella?"

Before her mind realized what she was doing, her body and heart had already made the call. Her school bag, with his gift of roses, slid off her shoulder as she let go of his arm to, finally, put her own arms around him. She could reach his shoulders, his neck; she had to stand on tiptoes and force his head down with all her might. And it worked.

She kissed him.

She didn't think about it anymore. She just moved as she had always wanted to. She ran her hands over his back and his thick hair; she used her tongue to taste him, his lips, the inside of his mouth. The rest of her followed; her chest and her hips pressed against him, wanting more, maybe at least for him to touch her, too.

He understood.

She knew as much when he came to life, knowing exactly what she wanted, what she needed.

His lips moved against hers; his tongue was deliciously soft and snake-like as it twisted its way into the depths of her mouth. His hands were all over her. His fingers ran through her long hair, his palms burned a path through her skin as he wrapped his arms around her waist and started caressing her buttocks. It wasn't very long until she was pressed against him so tightly, she could feel him, hard and insistent, against her own softness. His fingertips glided inside her skirt as he lifted one of her legs to wrap around his hip.

She gasped when he touched that part of her, expertly reaching inside the modest underwear she wore with her school uniform. His fingers rubbed and stroked her as she moaned against his chest.

She denied herself the pleasure that was beginning to build and decided to come back up for air. She grabbed at his arms, still feeling him against her.

"Take me home, Trey," she whispered into the night. "Make me yours."

He was always more at ease in the shadows. She watched as he picked up her things with ruthless efficiency. This time, it was his turn to take her hand and lead the way.

He lived in a warehouse, one filled with auto parts. The

lighting was sparse; except for a few fluorescent bulbs, it was the lights of the pier that danced with the shadows. He locked the door behind him and led her to a tiny corner where stood a small table, a portable chest of plastic drawers, a tiny refrigerator, and his bed, wooden, with a thin mattress on top.

He did not say anything; neither did she. He brought her to the bed and made her stand before him. He undressed her then, unbuttoning her blouse and skirt first and sliding them off of her. He fumbled a bit with her bra, but when he finally undid the clasp and took it off, she blushed deeply as he brought his lips to her nipples and suckled them hungrily. She would have fallen to the floor, easily, had it not been for his firm grip around her body.

When he was done, he lowered her stockings and panties and, before she could protest, his lips, his tongue and his hands were on her, all over her. After a few moments, he lifted her to the bed, settling her gently on her back. His mouth came down between her legs again, as did his fingers, and she was at his mercy. She called his name, bucked her hips, spread herself further, dug her nails into his shoulders, until he brought her to the peak and she heard herself scream and moan in pleasure.

"You are so beautiful." She heard him speak huskily, from somewhere above her. It took a few seconds for her eyes to focus as she came down from what she knew was her first climax. She had read about it in romance novels, seen it in movies that made her blush, and even heard girls with boyfriends talk about it, but she had never expected it to feel like this.

She had never expected she would feel it with him.

In what little light there was, she could see him next to her on the bed, his dark eyes almost disappearing into the shadows. He was still fully clothed.

"Oh." Embarrassment sank in for the first time. Her hands came up, to cover her utter lack of modesty, but his fingertips were on her face before she could reach for something, like a blanket or pillow, to cover up with.

"You don't have to hide. Never from me." For the first time, she heard a tremble in his voice. She could barely see his face. His fingertips were gentle as he traced her cheeks; the skin on his hands was hard, rough and warm. She could smell herself in his touch.

She reached for him. Before she could wrap her arms around him again, he caught her wrists.

"I think it's time for you to go home." There it was again, the shakiness in his voice. "I'll walk you there." He slowly let her go.

"No," she said, trying to lift her torso, to get a better look at him. "I want to stay with you."

He hesitated, then sat up, the cot creaking under his weight. "This is your…first time, isn't it?"

"Yes." Was there something she had done he didn't like? "What does that have to do with anything?"

"This is the biggest mistake you could ever make." His

back was as stiff and unyielding as a mountain, his voice low and almost menacing.

"Mistake? Who made you responsible for my decisions?" Heat rushed to her cheeks and forehead. She grabbed at the thin striped blanket folded under the pillow she had been lying on and hastily wrapped it around her nakedness.

"Decision? You call this a decision? To sleep with me?"

"To be with you, Trey." She was close to tears. She slid off the bed and got to her feet. He still had his back turned to her. At least he couldn't see her so disheveled and hurt. "I want to be with you. It was my choice to make. Don't you dare tell me you didn't want it, too. I felt it. Don't you fucking dare deny it."

He put his hands on his thick legs and rose, almost painstakingly. "I'm not denying anything." He turned slowly, running his fingers through his hair, which had become half-unbound after their kisses. He kept his eyes hooded, gaze to the floor, or at least not on her.

"I've never wanted a woman as much as I want you. Look at you, Stella. How could I or any man say no to you?"

"Then don't."

"If only it were that simple. If only I were any other man."

"You will never be any other man," she said, almost impatiently. "Look at you, Trey. How could any man compare to you?"

"Any other man wouldn't leave you." It was almost a whisper.

That stopped her.

"Then come back." Her lips finally uttered the very thing her heart had known for a long time. "When all this is over, come back to me."

As soon as she finished saying the words, a lone tear slid down the corner of her left eye, landing and splashing on her naked shoulder. She was terrified he saw it.

That was the last shred of her dignity.

Somehow, that was also the last shred of his control.

As long as it took her to blink back more tears, he closed the distance between them. The way he grabbed hold of her around the waist was almost bone-breaking, crushing the breath out of her. His lips came down on hers like a clap of thunder, as powerful and overwhelming as he.

Her flimsy cover of a blanket fell to the floor, just as she gave him her complete surrender. This time, there was no waiting, no caressing, no gentleness, as she kissed him back like a woman starved.

Dimly, she felt her hands rip away at the last barriers between them, his clothing. It didn't take long for him to be just as naked as she. He looked beautifully inhuman in the dim light and shifting shadows; his skin was smooth where there were no scars, but he had dozens of them all over his body, mixed with what looked and felt like burn marks. His hair fell on her face like a velvet curtain, scented by the sea and his sweat.

They didn't even make it to the bed, or at least she did, halfway. He was inside her, a perfect fit, buried completely, as her legs went around his waist, his shadow looming over her. She felt him thrusting faster and harder by the second, heard him say her name again and again, and, finally, asked her to look at him.

Their eyes locked briefly, and she drowned at the ferocity and desire she saw in the way he looked at her, and his lips were on hers again. He thrust the hardest then, and he shouted as his body shook as if he had a hundred earthquakes inside him, from inside her.

He collapsed, draped across her, his hair and sweat and breath on her breasts. She could feel a slick wetness burning straight from him into her.

Her heart was pounding so loudly she could barely hear anything else. She put her arms around him and kissed the top of his head, feeling only tenderness as she watched him looking spent and vulnerable.

Is this how it was supposed to feel?

She never had any more time to think about it that night. She could only feel, only him. They made love again, and again, and once more. He was insatiable, as if he wanted every last part of her for himself, but, to her surprise, so was she.

By dawn, he had touched and kissed every inch of her, and she of him. She was straddling him, arms around his neck, his teeth and tongue on her nipples, when she saw the first strains of light filter in through the high windows of the warehouse. By the time she came in his embrace, moaning his name, morning was upon them.

He was on his back and she sprawled on top of him, nuzzling his chest, when she realized it was the first time she was seeing him in the light of day.

"Come back to me, Trey," she blurted out, afraid he would somehow disappear. "No matter what happens, just come back to me."

He didn't respond, not for a long time. His arms went around her, so tightly, so protectively. She felt his lips on her temple, his heartbeat in her ear, his hands in her hair. She took these in, every touch, every scent, every sound, every feeling.

"I love you, Stella," he finally said.

PRISON

I love you.

After he said the words, he slowly moved her to the bed and wrapped her in his blanket. She watched him dress in his usual dark clothing and take only a black backpack.

"It's yours now," he said, giving her the keys he had used the night before. "Do whatever you like."

Before she could protest, he brought his arms around her and kissed her deeply. With one last caress on her cheek and her hair, he was gone.

Trey.

She didn't even know his last name.

Stella got out of his bed, dressed and gathered her things. It was only when she finished locking up the warehouse that she felt the scalding pain in her throat, from last night, finally bubble to the surface, unleashing itself with her tears.

As she walked home, she didn't have the heart to check her phone, knowing that it was probably bursting with worried texts and missed calls from her mother. She would deal with it all later. All that mattered at the moment was she make it through the pain, see herself home alive.

She had no idea how hard she had been clutching his box of roses in her hands. She was just about to cross the intersection when it fell from her grasp. The box burst open, spilling the three roses onto the street, along with a small rectangle of paper.

She crouched down and slowly gathered the fallen items, fitting them into her school bag, feeling spent and raw as she did. The rectangle turned out to be a business card, with something written on the back of it by hand. The name was familiar.

RAPHAEL I. ESGUERRA, III
CHIEF EXECUTIVE OFFICER
ESGUERRA HOLDINGS

Trey's boss. There was a number printed underneath, which looked oddly familiar. It took her a few seconds to figure out that the mobile phone number was Trey's. She had looked at his number and only message from last week so many times.

Why was his phone number on his boss' card?

At the back of the paper, in bold, slashing handwriting, was a short message.

Call whenever you need.

There will be an answer.

Trey

Unable to make sense of what she had just read, she fumbled with the rest of her things and slowly sat down at the bench by the intersection, taking deep breaths.

She slowly went back in memory, to what he had said in the time she was with him.

"Iloilo is our home, we were born and raised here. We won't give it up, so we're bringing the war to them."

"I work for the man who decided to put them there and, at the same time, get you out of something you wouldn't want."

"When I chose to do this, I knew I wouldn't be coming back."

"Some of us can't just quit. Some of us can't just give up the life we were born into."

Was Trey the boss he was referring to? Was he actually Raphael Esguerra?

Was he the Raphael Esguerra who protected her city?

Unable to stop herself, she took out her phone. The screen showed eighteen missed calls and almost double in unread messages. The battery was down to twelve percent.

She scrolled through her contacts, found Trey's number, and called it. She felt an icy chill envelop her body, despite the warmth of the morning sun.

Her call was picked up after two rings.

"Hello, Miss Montero. Good morning." The voice was different, older, female. It sounded almost like her own mother's voice.

"Hello," Stella echoed. She suddenly felt disoriented. "Who's this? Is Trey there?"

"My name is Rhoda, Miss Montero. I work for Mister Esguerra. Is there something I can do for you?"

"Where's Trey? I want to talk to him. Please."

"I believe he has informed you he will be indisposed. He has given us instructions to be at your service, as and when you need."

Us? Her brain tried to cope with the words of the woman at the other end of the line. *At her service?*

Wherever Trey was, she had already gotten her answer.

"No, thanks," she heard herself say. "I just wanted to give him back the keys to his… house."

"Did you? I was under the impression he has given them to you, to access and use the warehouse as you please."

"No. Yes. I didn't understand what he was trying to tell me."

There was a pause from Rhoda. "Is there anything else you need, Miss Montero? I can send a car for you if you need to get somewhere, wherever you are in the city."

To her horror, Stella felt a few tears slowly escape her already stinging, sleepless eyes. "I don't need a car. I'll walk home."

"Very well, Miss Montero. Please call me if you need anything, anything at all."

"Goodbye, Rhoda." Stella disconnected the call. She mechanically picked up her bag and stood up. She could feel her legs extend unwillingly, still sore from her night with him. She was beyond tired.

Raphael Esguerra.

A powerful name, feared and respected in the world she lived in.

Trey.

The man who moved in and out of the shadows and into her life, into her darkest dreams and desires.

They were the same person. The only man she had given her heart and her body to.

She would have given anything to make him stay. She knew, however, that no one could tell someone like Raphael Esguerra what to do.

The very same person who told her he loved her.

She had never said she loved him, too, had she? Loved him the moment she first laid eyes on him all those years ago, stepping out of the darkness, under the bright neon lights of a street corner.

It was the only regret she had. It was a prison she willingly put her heart into.

She carried this regret in the days, weeks and months that followed, silently, guardedly.

When she reached home that Saturday morning, instead of greeting her with panic or anger, her mother told her that she received a visitor named Rhoda, the mother of one of Stella's classmates, earlier that morning. Rhoda had apologized for not calling to tell her that Stella was helping her daughter with an urgent term paper, help given at the last minute to a desperate classmate. After breakfast in a fast food restaurant with her daughter, Stella would be home.

She went to the movies that evening with her friends. On Monday, the student council started putting up posters for the senior prom, scheduled on Valentine's Day. She wasn't surprised to get asked by Darryl, whom she politely turned down. In the weeks that followed, she refused four more invitations.

It was almost Christmas when she first heard about it on the news.

It was hard to miss. A large explosion in Sampaloc, Manila had taken down almost four blocks of factories and warehouses. A hundred injured, twenty dead. Up to and until Christmas, there were interviews of a bereaved widow named Connie Zamora, clutching a brood of four children, mourning the death of her husband, business magnate Michael Zamora. Connie demanded justice for her family and the families of their employees.

The media and the police suspected terrorists trying to

make a statement. Stella always looked at the sketches released to the public, but never found one she recognized.

Over the school break that December, just before New Year, she went back to the warehouse, on a quiet weekday evening.

It was the same way she had left it. She tidied up the bed, willing herself not to think of the person she had shared it with, and stripped the sheets for washing. She went through the plastic drawers and the refrigerator. The fridge had a few bottles of water and an unopened Snickers chocolate bar. The drawers contained an assortment of black and grey shirts, a few pairs of dark jeans, and shorts of different colors. All the clothes had been washed and neatly folded. In the bottom drawer was a plain ruled notebook and a few pencils. Nothing was written inside the notebook; there were only sketches that filled the pages, drawn in a neat, meticulous hand.

They were all sketches of her.

She spent the next hour crying on his bare mattress.

In January, she walked the runway for the first time, in a Dinagyang Festival fashion show. The designer was so impressed that she offered to design Stella's gown for the latter's senior prom, as part of her Valentine's Day portfolio.

February came with typhoons, one after the other. The rain on Valentine's Day reminded Stella of that night two years ago when the city was flooded.

The prom was at a seaside resort across town, in a covered pavilion with tall, thick glass windows that overlooked the beach. In spite of the weather, almost all her classmates and their dates had come.

Stella arrived with two other senior girls who didn't have escorts like her. All three of them lived in the same area and had opted to travel to and from the event together.

She made a stop at the bathroom before entering the venue. Pictures of the night were very important, according to the designer. They had contracted one of the prom photographers to take additional photos of her wearing the new dress.

The gown was made of deep red velvet, the color of blood. The neckline was cut low, off the shoulders, with small crisscrossing straps around her upper arms. The rest of the fabric was molded to her bodice and hips, then came apart by her left thigh in a slit, showing off her long legs, with the hemline almost brushing the floor.

The hairdresser had styled her hair half down, half up. It fell in waves all the way to the middle of her bare back. She had asked for three small roses to be put around the loose ponytail on top of her head. One red, one pink, one white.

'I love you, Stella.'

The words had echoed in her mind, heart and soul countless times since she heard them, for the first, only and, possibly, last time.

Staring back at her in the mirror was the very image of a romantic heroine, draped in the colors of love.

But she wasn't that heroine.

She was Stella Montero, who didn't even have a date to the prom. She didn't have someone special. She already had something more than that.

She already had her prison.

STORM

The prom was meant to last past midnight. The weather had other plans.

At nearly eleven that evening, Stella stood next to the glass door of the pavilion and looked up. She couldn't see any of the stars. The sky was almost completely covered in thick clouds. There was only the moon, cutting through the dark shroud with tiny yet sharp slivers of light.

The rain fell in a steady downpour, the winds picking up in speed with each hour that passed. A full-blown storm would be upon them soon.

She had spent the past few hours having her picture taken and getting congratulated by practically everyone present: her teachers, classmates and schoolmates, even visitors from other schools. She was, apparently, the frontrunner for Prom Queen.

She was not surprised when someone from the student council came over to escort her across the dance floor. It was the treasurer, a classmate of hers since freshman year named Vic. He guided her up the small stage and led her to a spot in a line where three other girls stood. Vic winked at her and mouthed, *"Congratulations. It's you."*

In one corner of the platform stood the male half of the prom court. Darryl already had the Prom King crown on his head. He was flanked by three other boys from her class who wore blue sashes as the first, second and third princes.

The emcee, a deejay from a popular local radio station, came forward dramatically, brandishing an important-looking cream-colored envelope. He took out a card of the same color and began to read out the names of the third and second princesses.

Stella felt the hug of the last girl standing next to her seconds after she heard her name being called as Prom Queen. The president of the student council came forward and put a pink and gold sash over her shoulder, followed by the college dean who pinned a bejeweled tiara to her hair. She was hugged and kissed by a few more people before Darryl stood in front of her bearing a bouquet of white, yellow and pink flowers, mostly roses. Photographers surged forward and snapped pictures at an alarming, blinding rate.

She could hear the strains of David Pomeranz's song, 'King and Queen of Hearts,' coming over the speakers. This was the traditional Prom King and Queen dance.

The crowd applauded. The catcalls, whistles and whoops were deafening.

The skies responded, splitting open with a resounding, bright burst of lightning. Thunder followed, echoing through the sudden darkness that blanketed the entire pavilion.

"The power just went out," she heard the deejay say loudly. "Everyone please stay calm."

Someone grabbed her hand, pulling her to the left side of the stage. She thought at first it was Darryl, but she was certain he was on the opposite side of the stage, where moments before he stood under the spotlight with an obnoxious-looking bouquet in his hand and a silly grin on his face.

Stella found her voice, her hand instinctively going up to prevent the tiara on her head from falling. She could use it as a weapon, too, just in case.

"What the hell do you think you're doing?" she demanded.

"Hi, Stella." The voice came from the deepest shadows of stage left, the only sound she could hear clearly even with the rising din of people talking in the darkness.

She knew that voice.

"Trey?" she heard herself respond, in what sounded like a desperate whisper. Maybe she had completely lost it now.

Cellphones and lighters began coming to life on the pavilion floor, allowing her to see more clearly.

A single streak of light moved across the spot where she heard his voice coming from, falling on his profile for the briefest moment.

That was all she needed to see.

She unceremoniously pulled the errant tiara off her head and tossed it aside, then jumped off the stage and into his arms.

She landed on his chest, her fingers clutching the fabric

of his shirt, her face burrowing into his neck, desperately taking in his familiar scent of pine and the sea.

Trey's hands were warm on her back. He was raining kisses on her hair and face. She knew the feeling of his lips on her skin.

"Let's get out of here," she heard him say.

Nothing in the world could stop her from going with him. She was not sure if he carried her, or she ran alongside him, but she found herself in a hut at the farthest end of the resort, cloaked by the night and the rain.

Before them, the surf crashed roughly against the shore. Their shelter of dried woven leaves made little consequence. They were both soaked to the skin.

It was only when he stood still before her, in the pale, thin light of the moon, was she finally convinced he was real. She reached out and touched his face, taking in all the planes and angles.

"I missed you so much," she said. "Whoever you are."

"It doesn't matter who I am. It never mattered to you."

He was right. It never did.

"What matters is that I love you." The words came out easily, as naturally as she breathed in the salty air and the heady scent of him. She touched the scar on his right cheek. She watched as he turned his head and started kissing her fingertips.

"You are so beautiful." His voice was equal parts passionate and tender, as was his gaze.

"So are you," she said, as she traced his lips and jawline.

"I came back to you," he said. "Do you know what that means?"

She put her arms around his torso, angling her ear so she could hear his heartbeat. "That you really love me? That you missed me, too?"

"It means I am yours, Stella. I have been yours the moment I saw you sitting in that intersection. I couldn't stop thinking about you. I tried to draw you. I never thought I could even touch you. You're an angel on earth I would die to protect."

She could feel the tears welling up behind her eyes, from the flood of emotion that overcame her.

But she didn't have time for tears now.

She only had time for him, because she belonged to him, too.

She reached up and put her hands on his shoulders, the same way she had all those months ago. She didn't have to pull him down. He lifted her off her feet to kiss her.

"I am yours, too," she said against his lips. "*Raphael. Trey.*"

She let the names roll off her tongue. There was nothing strange about them. They were both him.

Stella kissed him, then, before she finally called him what she had really wanted to, all these years.

"*My angel.*"

About the Author

Shirley Siaton writes edgy and evocative stories and poems. Her worlds are in a deliciously dark cross-section of the romance, neo-noir, action, fantasy, new adult and contemporary genres.

She has several books of fiction and poetry released since February 2023. Her first book is the free verse collection *'Black Cat and other poems.'* She also pens juvenile literature as Shirley Parabia.

She is an award-winning writer, poet and journalist in English, Filipino and Hiligaynon, lauded by the Stevan Javellana Foundation, Philippine Information Agency and West Visayas State University. Her essays, short stories and poems have been published internationally in print and digital media. Her multi-lingual plays have been staged in the Philippines.

Shirley is a black belt in Shotokan Karate and an international certified fitness coach. Originally from Iloilo City, she is based in the Middle East with her husband and two daughters.

Links

Shirley's official website:
shirleysiaton.com

Complete reading guide:
shirley.pub

Subscribe to Shirley's VIP list for free exclusive updates:
newsletter.shirleysiaton.com

www.ingramcontent.com/pod-product-compliance
Lightning Source LLC
LaVergne TN
LVHW040917110526
838202LV00089B/3643